PENGUIN INTERNATIONAL WRITERS

MY FIRST LOVES

Ivan Klíma was born in 1931 in Prague, where he now lives. He was the editor of the journal of the Czech Writers' Union during the Prague Spring. In 1969 he was a visiting professor to the University of Michigan. He returned to Czechoslovakia the following year. Ivan Klíma has written plays, stories and novels, including *My Merry Mornings*, *A Summer Affair* (Penguin 1990), *Love and Garbage* (Penguin 1991) and *My Golden Trades* (1992). His work is published worldwide.

Ewald Osers was born in Prague in 1917 and has lived in England since 1938. He has won many awards for his translations, including the Schlegel-Tieck Prize in 1971, and is a Fellow of the Royal Society of Literature.

MY FIRST LOVES

Ivan Klíma

Translated from the Czech by Ewald Osers

PENGUIN BOOKS

PENGUIN BOOKS

Published by the Penguin Group
Penguin Books Ltd, 27 Wrights Lane, London W8 5TZ, England
Penguin Books USA Inc., 375 Hudson Street, New York, New York 10014, USA
Penguin Books Australia Ltd, Ringwood, Victoria, Australia
Penguin Books Canada Ltd, 10 Alcorn Avenue, Toronto, Ontario, Canada M4V 3B2
Penguin Books (NZ) Ltd, 182–190 Wairau Road, Auckland 10, New Zealand

Penguin Books Ltd, Registered Offices: Harmondsworth, Middlesex, England

First published in Sweden, under the title *Mina Första Kärlekar*, 1985
This translation first published in Great Britain by Chatto and Windus 1986
Published in Penguin Books 1989
10 9 8 7 6 5

Copyright © Ivan Klíma, 1985
Translation copyright © Ewald Osers, 1986
All rights reserved

Printed in England by Clays Ltd, St Ives plc

My First Loves

Miriam

My father's cousin was celebrating her engagement. Aunt Sylvia was short, had a large nose, and was suntanned and loquacious. Before the war she'd been a clerk in a bank; now she'd become a gardener, while her intended – originally a lawyer – was employed in the food supply office. Quite what his job there was I didn't know, but Father had promised us that there'd be a surprise at the party and he'd smacked his lips meaningfully, which aroused enthusiastic interest in my brother and me.

My aunt lived in the same barracks as us, in a tiny little room with a small window giving on to the corridor. The room was so small that I couldn't imagine what it had ever been intended for. Probably as a store for small items such as horseshoes, whips (the place used to be a cavalry barracks) or spurs. In that little room my aunt had a bed, and a small table made from two suitcases. Over the top suitcase she had now spread a tablecloth and laid out some open sandwiches on a few plates cut out of cardboard. They were genuine open sandwiches covered with pieces of salami, sardines, liver pâté, raw turnips, cucumbers and real cheese. Auntie had even prepared some small cakes with beet jam. I noticed my brother swallowing noisily as his mouth began to water. He hadn't learned to control himself yet. He'd never been to school. I had, and I was already reading about wily Ulysses and forgetful Paganel, so I knew something about gods and the virtues of men.

This was the first time I saw the fiancé. He was a young man with curly hair and round cheeks which bore no trace whatever of wartime hardships.

So we met in that little room with its blacked-out window.

Nine of us crowded into it and the air soon got stale and warm and laden with sweat, but we ate, we devoured the unimaginable goodies which the fiancé had clearly supplied from the food supply store, we washed down the morsels with ersatz coffee that smelled of milk and was beautifully sweet. At one point my father clinked his knife against his mug and declared that no time was so bad that something good mightn't occur in it; its many significant events – he would only list the defeat of the Germans at Sebastopol and the British offensive in Italy – now included this celebration. Father wished the happy couple to be able to set out on a honeymoon in freedom by the next month, he wished them an early peace and much happiness and love together. Better to be sad but loved, Father surprised everybody by quoting Goethe, than to be cheerful without love.

Then we sang a few songs and because supper was beginning to be doled out we had to bring the party to an end.

When I returned with my billycan full of beet bilge I saw the white-haired painter Speero – Maestro Speero, as everyone called him – sitting by one of the arched but unglazed window openings. He too had his billycan standing by his side – except that his was already empty – while on his lap he held a board to which he had fixed a piece of drawing paper. He was sketching. There were several artists living on our corridor but Maestro Speero was the oldest and most famous of them. In Holland, where he came from, he had designed medallions, banknotes and postage stamps, and even the Queen had allegedly sat for him. Here, although this was strictly forbidden, he sketched scenes from our ghetto on very small pieces of paper. The pictures were so tiny that it seemed impossible to me that these delicate lines were created by that elderly hand.

On one occasion I had plucked up my courage, put together all my knowledge of German and asked Herr Speero why he was drawing such very small pictures.

8

'Um sie besser zu verschlucken' – all the better to swallow them – he'd replied. But maybe I'd misunderstood him and he'd said 'verschicken' – to send – or even 'verschenken' – to give.

Now full of admiration I watched as his paper filled up with old men and women standing in line, all pressed together. They were no bigger than a grain of rice, but every one of them had eyes, a nose and a mouth, and on their chest the Jewish star. As I stared intently at his paper it seemed to me that the tiny figures began to run around, swarming over the picture like ants, till my head swam and I had to close my eyes.

'Well, what do you think?' the white-haired artist asked without turning his head.

'Beautiful,' I breathed. Not for anything in the world would I have admitted to him that I too had tried to people pieces of paper with tiny figures, that in my sunnier moments, when I allowed myself a future outside the area bounded by the ramparts, I pictured myself in some witness-bearing occupation – as a poet, an actor or a painter. Suddenly a thought struck me. 'May I offer you some soup?'

Only then did the old man turn to me. 'What's that?' he asked in surprise. 'Have they dished out seconds already? Or are you sick?'

'My aunt's got married,' I explained.

Herr Speero picked up his billycan from the ground, there wasn't a drop left in it, and I poured into it more than half my helping of the beet bilge. He bowed a little and said: 'Thank you, thank you very much for this token of favour. God will reward you.'

Except, where is God, I reflected in the evening as I lay on my palliasse which was infested with bedbugs and visited by fleas, and how does he reward good deeds? I could not imagine him, I could not imagine hope beyond this world.

And this world?

9

Every evening I would anxiously strain my ears for sounds in the dark. For the sound of boots down the corridor, for a desperate scream shattering the silence, for the sudden opening of a door and the appearance of a messenger with a slip of paper with my name typed on it. I was afraid of falling asleep, of being caught totally helpless. Because then I wouldn't be able to hide from him.

I had thought up a hiding place for myself in the potato store in the basement. I would wriggle through my narrow window, after locking-up time, and bury myself so deep among the potatoes that no SS man would see me and no dog get scent of me. The potatoes would keep me alive.

How long could a person live on raw potatoes? I didn't know, but then how much longer could the war last? Yes, that was what everything depended on.

I knew that fear would now creep out from the corner by the stove. All day long it was hiding out there, cowering in the flue or under the empty coal-bucket, but once everybody was asleep it would come to life, pad over to me and breathe coldly on my forehead. And its pale lips would whisper: woe . . . be-tide . . . you.

Quietly I got off my palliasse and tiptoed to the window. I knew the view well: the dark crowns of the ancient lime-trees outside the window, the brick gateway with its yawning black emptiness. And the sharp outlines of the ramparts. Cautiously I lifted a corner of the black-out paper and froze: the top of one of the lime-trees was aglow with a blue light. A spectral light, cold and blinding. I stared at it for a moment. I could make out every single leaf, every little glowing twig, and I became aware at the same time that the branches and the leaves were coming together in the shape of a huge, grinning face which gazed at me with flaming eyes.

I felt I was choking and couldn't have cried out even had I dared to do so. I let go of the black paper and the window was once more covered in darkness. For a while I stood there motionless and wrestled with the temptation to lift the paper again and get another glimpse of that face. But I lacked the courage. Besides, what was the point? I could see that face before me, shining through the black-out, flickering over the dark ceiling, dancing in front of my eyes even when I firmly closed my eyelids.

What did it mean? Who did it belong to? Did it hold a message for me? But how would I know whether it was good news or bad?

By morning nothing was left of the joys or the fears of the night before. I went to get my ration of bitter coffee, I gulped down two slices of bread and margarine. I registered with relief that the war had moved on by one night and that the unimaginable peace had therefore drawn another night nearer.

I went behind the metal-shop to play volleyball, and an hour before lunchtime I was already queuing up with my billycan for my own and my brother's eighth-of-a-litre of milk. The line stretched towards a low vaulted room, not unlike the one inhabited by Aunt Sylvia. Inside, behind an iron pail, stood a girl in a white apron. She took the vouchers from the submissive queuers, fished around in the pail with one of the small measures and poured a little of the skimmed liquid into the vessels held out to her.

As I stood before her she looked at me, her gaze rested on my face for a moment, and then she smiled. I knew her, of course, but I hadn't really taken proper notice of her. She had dark hair and a freckled face. She bent over her metal pail again, took my mug, picked up the largest of the measures, dipped it into the huge bucket and emptied its contents into my mug. Hurriedly she added two more helpings, then she returned my mug and smiled at me again. As if by her smile she were trying to tell me something significant, as if she were touching me with it. She returned my mug full to the brim and I mumbled my thanks. I didn't understand anything. I was not used to receiving strangers' smiles or any kind of tokens of favour. Out in the corridor I leaned against the wall and, as though I were afraid she might run after me and deprive me of that irregular helping, I began to drink. I drank at least two thirds of the milk, knowing full well that even so my brother would not be cheated.

In the evening, even before fear crept out from its corner, I tried to forestall it or somehow to delay it. I thought of that strange incident. I should have liked to explain it to myself, perhaps to connect it with the old artist's ceremonial thanks and hence with the working of a superior power, but I decided not to attach such importance to my own deed. But what did last night's fiery sign mean? Abruptly it emerged before my eyes, its glow filling me with a chill. Could that light represent something good?

I made myself get up from my palliasse and breathlessly lifted the corner of the black-out.

Outside the darkness was undisturbed, the black top of the lime-tree was swaying in the gusts of wind, clouds were scurrying across the sky, their edges briefly lit by summer lightning.

Next day I was filled with impatience as I stood in the queue, gripping my clean mug. It took me a considerable effort to dare to look at her face. She had large eyes, long and almond-shaped and almost as dark as ersatz coffee. She smiled at me, perhaps she even winked at me conspiratorially – I wasn't sure. Into my mug she poured three full measures and handed it back to me as if nothing were amiss. Outside the door I drank up three quarters of my special ration, watching other people come out with mugs whose bottoms were barely covered by the white liquid. I still didn't understand anything. I drifted down the long corridor, covering my mug with my other hand. Even after I'd finished drinking there was an embarrassing amount left in it. And she'd smiled at me twice.

I was beginning to be filled with a tingling, happy excitement.

In the evening, as soon as I'd closed my eyes, I saw my flaming sign again, that glowing face, but this time it had lost its menace and rapidly took on a familiar appearance. I could make out the minute freckles above the upper lip; I recognized the mouth half-parted in a smile, the almond eyes looked at me with such a strange gaze that I caught my breath. Her eyes gazed on me with love.

Suddenly I understood the meaning of the fiery sign and the meaning of what was happening.

I was loved.

A mouse rustled in the corner, somewhere below a door banged, but the world receded and I was looking at a sweet face and felt my own face relax and my lips smile.

What can I do to see you, in the flesh, to see you here and now, and not just across a wooden table with a huge pail towering between us?

But what would I do if we really did meet?

By the next day, when I'd received my multiplied milk ration and when a gentle and expressive smile had assured me I wasn't mistaken, I could no longer bear the isolation of my feelings. I had at least to mention her to everybody I spoke to, and every mention further fanned my feelings. Moreover, I learned from friends that her name was Miriam Deutsch and that she lived on my floor, only at the other end. I even established the number of her room: two hundred and three. We also considered her age – some thought she was sixteen and others that she was already eighteen, and someone said he'd seen her twice with some Fred but it needn't mean anything.

Of course it didn't mean anything. I was sure no Fred came away with a full mug of milk every day. Besides, where would my beloved Miriam get so much from?

By now I knew almost everything about her, I could even visit her any time during the day and say . . . Well, what was I to say to her? What reason could I give for my intrusion? Some pretext! I might take along my grubby copy of the Story of the Trojan War.

I brought you this book for the milk!

Except that I must not say anything of the kind in front of

others. I might ask her to step out into the corridor with me. But suppose she said she had no time? Suppose I offended her by mentioning the milk? It seemed to me that it was improper to speak about tokens of love.

But suppose I was altogether wrong? Why should such a girl be in love with me, a scrawny, tousle-haired ragamuffin? I hadn't even started to grow a beard!

Right at the bottom of my case I had a shirt which I only wore on special occasions. It was canary-yellow and, unlike the rest of my shirts, it was as yet unfrayed about the collar and the cuffs. I put it on. All right, so it throttled me a little but I was prepared to suffer that. I also had a suit in my case but unfortunately I'd grown out of it. My mother had tried to lengthen the trouser legs but even so they only just reached my ankles and there was no material left to lengthen the arms. I hesitated for a moment but I had no choice. I took my shirt off again, poured some water into my washbowl and washed thoroughly. I even scrubbed my neck. When I'd put on my festive garb I wetted my hair and painstakingly made an exemplary parting. I half opened the window, held the black-out behind it, and for a while observed my image on the glass. In a sudden flush of self-love it seemed to me that I looked good the way I was dressed.

Then I set out along the long corridor to the opposite side of the barracks. I passed dozens of doors, the numbers above the hinges slowly going down. Two hundred and eighteen, two hundred and seventeen, two hundred and fifteen . . . I was becoming aware of the pounding of my heart.

Miriam. It seemed to me that I had never heard a sweeter name. It suited her. Two hundred and seven. I still didn't know what I was actually going to do. If she loved me – two hundred and six, good Lord, that's her door already over there, I can see it now – if she loves me the way I love her she'll come out and we'll meet – two hundred and five, I've slowed down to give her more time. The door will open and she will stand in it, and she'll smile at me: Where have you sprung from?

Oh, I just happened to be walking past. Meeting the chaps on the ramparts, usually walk across the yard.

I stopped. A stupid sentence, that. Why couldn't I have thought of something cleverer?

Hi, Miriam!

You know my name?

I just had to find out. So I could think of you better.

You think of me?

Morning till night, Miriam! And at night too. I think of you nearly all through the night!

I think of you too. But where have your sprung from?

I don't really know. Suddenly occurred to me to go this way rather than across the yard.

That seemed a little better. Two hundred and four.

You see I live on the same floor.

So we're really almost neighbours. You could always walk along this way.

I will. I will.

Two hundred and three. I drew a deep breath. I stared at the door so intently that it must surely sigh deep down in its wooden soul. And she, if she loved me, must get up, walk to her door and come out.

Evidently she wasn't there. Why should she be sitting at home on a fine afternoon? Maybe she'll be coming back from somewhere, I just have to give her enough time. Two hundred and two. I was approaching one of the transversal corridors which linked the two longitudinal wings of the barracks. I heard some clicking footsteps coming along it.

Great God Almighty! I stopped and waited with bated breath.

Round the corner appeared an old woman in clogs. In her hands she was carrying a small dish with a few dirty potatoes in it. Supper was obviously being doled out already.

The next day I saw Miriam again behind the low table with the iron pail full of milk. She took my mug and smiled at me, one helping, a second, a third, she smiled again and handed me my mug. How I love you, Miriam, nobody can have ever felt anything like it. I leaned against the wall, drank two thirds of the message of love and returned to my realm of dreams.

I didn't emerge from it till towards the evening, when the women were coming back from work. I washed, straightened my parting, put on my special suit, but I felt that this was not enough. I lacked a pretext for my festive attire, for our meeting, and even more so for telling her something about myself.

Just then I remembered an object of pride, a proof of my skill. It was lying hidden and carefully packed away in the smaller case under my bunk: my puppet theatre. I had made it out of an old box, painted the stage sets on precious cartridge paper saved from school, made most of the various props from bits of wood, stones and small branches collected under the ramparts, while I'd made the puppets from chestnuts, cotton-reels and rags I'd scrounged from my mother and others living around us.

I took the box out of my case. It was tied up with twisted-paper ribbon. The proscenium arch, the wings and the rest of the scenery, the props and the puppets – they were all inside.

Hi, Miriam!

Hi, where have you sprung from?

Going to see a chap. We're going to perform a play.

You perform plays?

Only with puppets. For the time being.

How do you mean: for the time being?

One day I'll be an actor. Or a writer. I also think up plays.

You can do that?

Sure. I pick up some puppets and just start playing. I don't know myself how it's going to end.

And you play to an audience?

As large a one as you like. I'm not nervous.

And where did you get that theatre from?

Made it myself.

The scenery too?

Sure. I paint. If I have enough cartridge paper. I've done our barracks and the metal-shop and the gateway when a transport's just passing through . . .

I tied the ribbon round the box again. It looked perfectly ordinary, it might contain anything – like dirty washing. I undid the ribbon once more, pushed two puppets out so their little feet in their clogs were peeping out under the lid, as well as the king's head with its crown on, and then I tied the box up again. Then I set out along the familiar corridor.

I've also written a number of poems, I confided.

You write poetry? What about?

Oh, various things. About love. About suicide.

You tried to kill yourself?

No, not me. Two hundred and ten. My breath was coming quickly. A man mustn't kill himself.

Why mustn't he?

It's a sin!

You believe in that sort of thing?

What sort of thing?

God!

Two hundred and seven. Dear Lord, if you exist make her come out. Make her show herself. She doesn't even have to say any of these things, just let her smile.

You believe in him?

I don't know. They're all saying that if he existed he wouldn't allow any of this.

But you don't think so?

Maybe it's some punishment, Miriam.

Punishment for what?

Only he knows that. Two hundred and four. I stopped and transferred the box from my left arm to my right. Suppose I just dropped it and spilled everything? It would make a noise and I could pretend that I was picking up the

17

strewn pieces. I could kneel there for half an hour, picking things up.

Miriam, come out and smile at me. Nothing more. I swear that's all I want.

The following day she took my mug but I wasn't sure whether she'd smiled as warmly as the day before. I was alarmed. Suppose she didn't love me any longer? Why should she still love me when I couldn't summon up enough courage to do anything? Here she was giving me repeated proof of her favour and what was I doing?

One measure, a second, a third, a smile after all, the mug handed back to me – how I love you, Miriam. My divine Aphrodite, it's only that I'm too shy to tell you but nobody can ever love you as much as I do. Because I love you unto death, my Miriam!

In the evening they began to come round with deportation slips. And after that every day. Never before had such doom descended upon our ghetto. Thousands of people were shuffling towards the railway station with little slips on their chests.

And meanwhile every afternoon three helpings of promise, three helpings as a token of love, three helpings of hope. I returned to my room and prayed. Devoutly, for all my dear ones and for all distant ones, but especially for her, for Miriam, asking God to be merciful towards her and not to demand her life; and they called up all my friends and most of the people I knew by sight, the cook from the cookhouse and the man who handed out the bread. Corridors and yards fell silent, the streets were empty, the town was dead. On the last transport went my father's cousin, short Aunt Sylvia, along with her husband who'd worked in the food supply office. They'd barely been together three weeks and this was to have been their honeymoon trip in freedom. But perhaps, I tried to remember my father's words, it was better to suffer and be loved than to be joyous without love: I was only just beginning to understand the meaning of the words he'd quoted from the

18

poet. A few more days of anxiety in case the messengers appeared again, but they didn't, and the two of us remained behind! Now I won't hesitate any more, now at last I'll summon up my courage. While the terror lasted I couldn't speak of love, it wouldn't have been right, but now I can and must. I'll no longer walk past her door but I'll address her here and now, on the spot, as she returns my mug to me.

This evening at six, under the arch of the rear gateway – do please come, Miriam.

No!

You will come, Miriam, won't you?

No!

Could I see you some time, Miriam? How about this evening at six by the rear gateway? You will come, won't you?

The queue was shortening, there was hardly anyone left now with a claim to a mouthful of milk.

My knees were almost giving way, I hoped I wouldn't be scared at the last moment by my own boldness. She had my mug in her hand, I opened my mouth, one scoop, not the big one, the smallest one. As for her, she was looking at me without smiling. Could it be she didn't recognize me? I swallowed hard, at last she smiled, a little sadly, almost apologetically, and returned my mug to me, its bottom spattered with a revoltingly blueish, watery liquid. But this is me, Miriam, me who . . .

I took the mug from her hand and walked back down the long corridor at whose end, in front of the arched window, the famous Dutchman was again sitting with his squared paper.

What was I to do now?

I was still walking but I noticed that I wasn't really moving, I wasn't getting any nearer to the famous painter – on the contrary – and everything around me was beginning to move. I saw the old man rocking on his little chair as if being tossed about by waves, I saw him changing into

19

his own picture and saw the picture floating on the surface of the churned-up water.

I didn't know what was happening to me. All I knew was that she no longer loved me. A sickeningly sweet taste spread in my mouth, my cheeks were withering rapidly, and so were my hands. I was only just aware that I couldn't hold the light, almost empty, mug and I heard the metal ring against the stone floor of the corridor.

When I came round I saw above me the elderly face of Maestro Speero. With one hand he was supporting my back, while the other was moving a cold, wet cloth across my forehead. 'What's up boy?' he asked.

It took me a moment to return fully to merciless reality. But how could I reveal the real cause of my grief?

'They've taken my aunt away,' I whispered. 'Had to join the deportation transport. The one who got married.'

Mr Speero shook his white head. 'God be with her,' he said softly, 'and with all of us.'

My Country

We got off the train at a small station in the middle of the woods. Mother wore a tired and long-suffering expression, Father was dragging two huge suitcases and tried to reassure us with a smile. My brother and I also carried a case each, and we were curious to see what would happen next.

The landscape, as far as the eye could see, was as flat as a pancake. That suited me very well because you can move about more quickly on flat ground. I had no time for climbing any mountains. The reason was that I'd taken with me five massive tomes by the great masters of world literature and I was determined to read them in the shortest possible time. Besides I'd been instructed to see life for myself.

Just then Father noticed an ox-cart standing outside the station, in the charge of a ginger-haired youth. He immediately planted his cases by Mother's feet, ordered us all to guard them, and ran off towards the man who commanded what appeared to be the only local means of transport.

I was, at the time, passing through an important phase of my life. For the past few weeks I had known what I wanted. Of this vacation and of life itself.

What had happened a few weeks before was this. I had brought my Czech teacher a few literary attempts of my own (they were for the most part concerned with my wartime experiences) and she, either from embarrassment or from misplaced pride, had sent them to the editor of a cultural periodical. The editor of the journal, a lady, thereupon turned up at our school one morning. The two ladies had me summoned to the staff room, where they talked to me affably and seriously. The editor declared that from what she'd read she could see that I was a perceptive and sensitive boy who'd gone through a lot and had a need to communicate it.

Her words gave me a delicious thrill and even my white-haired, spinsterish Czech schoolmistress smiled at me encouragingly.

But now, the editor continued, she would advise me to try to put my wartime experiences out of my mind for a while and to observe life attentively and humbly, and get to know it. And I'd have to read, attentively and humbly read the great masters of world literature, such as Balzac, Stendhal, Maupassant, Gorky and Sholokhov. And, of course, reflect on what I'd read and observe how marvellously those authors mastered their craft. This would be the best way for me to learn how to write and, maybe, follow in their footsteps.

Then she got up, ceremoniously shook hands with me and said she was sure she'd hear more about me. I didn't in the least appreciate that she had just dismissed my literary efforts as clumsy, and I made an on-the-spot decision. I would be a writer, I would constantly observe life, and the rest of the time I'd read the great masters of world literature.

Father returned from the ox-cart and the smile on his face told us he had good news.

By an odd chance that man was the very person we wanted. His name was Pavelec, he had a farm, and on that farm there was a well, and in the well a pump driven by a new electric motor. At the words electric motor my mother as usual began to frown, while Father continued to explain that the motor – a 'Darling' by make – had broken down the previous week. Father believed he could put it right easily enough and would no doubt have gone on to tell us more about the new pump if he hadn't noticed that Mother was on the point of collapsing, and so he merely added that Mr Pavelec had a splendid room with three beds in it, and that he was willing to let it to us.

'But there are four of us!' Mother quite rightly objected.

Father smiled and said that it would all be dealt with. Besides, there was an inn in the village where the food was excellent.

'And suppose they've got mice?' Mother voiced an objection to the room on Mr Pavelec's farm.

Father assured her that in that case we'd immediately leave the farm, but the thought made Mother put on an even longer-suffering face. Then we piled our cases on the cart and set out in the direction of the village which had the poetical name of St Marie.

Less than an hour later Father was happily kneeling in front of the stripped-down electric motor, Mother was peering suspiciously under the massive, rustic bed checking for traces of mice, while Mr Pavelec was walking with me to the nearby inn, where we would take all our meals and where a bed might perhaps be found for me.

The inn was called the Štěrbák Inn, evidently after its owner, and proclaimed its name in bright-red letters on a white board. A smaller board announced, under the green mouth of a fish, that

> We serve breakfast, lunch and dinner;
> Every meal's a real winner.
> If you have a taste for fish
> You can't afford to miss our dish!

We entered and were immediately met by a man with a pencil behind his ear; he flashed his gold teeth at us and shook hands with Mr Pavelec. Over his black trousers he wore a blue-and-white apron which did not quite succeed in hiding his massive pot-belly.

'So this young man needs a room?' Mr Štěrbák said, referring to me. 'Well, we might put him into Number 5, next to the doctor's wife.'

The stairs we climbed were steep and scrubbed white. At the top, on a small landing, I saw five doors. Above the one Mr Štěrbák unlocked hung a wooden crucifix.

23

Inside the door there was a smell of soap and quinces. The feather duvet was so fat that it projected above the half-metre wooden sides.

I was delighted. I put my suitcase down by the side of a little table with a brilliant white cover and got ready to unpack my things, that is mainly my books, at once. But then I couldn't resist the temptation after all and went over to the window. Directly in front of me was the majestically spreading top of a chestnut-tree. Under it a few tables and folding chairs gleamed red. The fence was close-boarded and overgrown with shrubs. A small back-door opened on to a path leading down to the river. As I could see from my vantage point, the river here formed two arms which enclosed an oblong, grassy island linked to our bank by a foot-bridge. A little way beyond it, where the two arms met again, the water fell over a low weir.

On the island and on the near bank brightly-coloured little figures were scurrying about. A girl in a leaf-green swimsuit climbed up a smooth boulder on the bank and dived from it into the water.

Out on the landing a door slammed and a girl's voice shouted at somebody to get a move on. As a proper observer of life I should have opened my door and established who owned the voice, but I felt too shy.

Instead I lifted the lid of my case and took out all my books. Provided the weather, after six or seven cloudless weeks of sunshine, became reasonable at last and turned to rain, I'd easily manage to read them all.

I chose one of the books and tried to stretch out on the bed.

In the room next door a deep alto voice started laughing. Then something creaked, probably a wardrobe door, and a moment later I could hear water being poured into a washbowl. This intrigued me so much that I put my book down and listened carefully.

For a while there was some splashing of water, then a door clicked and from the landing came the sound of light, unquestionably female, footsteps.

I had of course brought along with me some blank paper and several exercise books in black covers in case I felt like doing some writing, as well as pencils, a fountain pen, an ordinary pen with nib and a small bottle of ink. I pretended to myself that I was unpacking these items but then I crossed to the window and waited.

After a short while a fair-haired, suntanned woman in a pale-chicory dress appeared on the path that ran through the meadow to the river. She was carrying a beach-bag. She moved briskly, without turning her head, so that I did not see her face. I was about to leave my observation post when two young girls burst out of the house in clothes of the same colour and with a lot of shouting ran down the path. The woman stopped and turned towards them, and hence also towards me, but she was too far away for me to make out her features.

The great master Maxim Gorky wrote:

'Sing or you die!' shouted Petrovsky and Lyoska flung out her arms wide and said: 'I've fallen in love with him, I'm saying it in front of everybody – I've fallen in love till my knees tremble.'

And a moment later all of them, insatiably, demanded something more.

I know that these are unworthy people, but they have a religious respect for beauty, they serve it to the point of total disregard for themselves, they get intoxicated by its poison and would be capable even of murdering for it.

From this conflict arises within me a flood of vague longings that stifle me. But in these people madness reaches its highest peak, although all songs have long been sung and all dances danced.

'Undress the women!' yelled Petrovsky.

It was always Stepanichin who undressed them. He did not hurry with his task, he carefully untied the tapes, undid the hooks and neatly folded the blouses, skirts and shirts. The men had a good look at Lyoska's body, carefully they touched her provocative breasts, her fine strong legs and her magnificent *belly, they walked round the women, sighing with admiration and glorying in their bodies with the same delight as they took in song and dance. Then they returned to the table in the small room, they ate and drank and – then began the indescribable spectacle of horror.*

Dinner was served in a small dining-room with only six tables. At the neighbouring table I immediately noticed the fair-haired lady with the two young girls. At first glance she was a lady, at least insofar as ladies differ from ordinary women by their pieces of jewellery, their silk clothes, painted lips and a proud way of holding their heads. Her head was round and on the small side, her eyes were the same colour as her dress. With them at the table sat a horsey-looking fellow. As our family sat down, the fellow stood up, flashed his teeth which fitted perfectly into his horse's mouth (they were yellow, blunt and massive, and well suited to the chewing of hay), held out his hand to Father (with a middle finger yellow from tar and nicotine, or whatever discolours the fingers of smokers) and announced that he was Dr Slavík from Prague-Dejvice and those folk over there were his family: his wife Paula and twins Millie and Rosie. Father in return declared that he was an engineer, also from Prague, that he had constructed a welding tool which the doctor was bound to have seen somewhere, that I was a seventh-form student (in fact I'd only just finished the fifth form so that, surprisingly, Father for once was only one year out) and that his other son, meaning my brother, was still a child. He didn't mention Mother because he knew that Mother was suspicious of all strangers and more particularly, ever since she had been misdiagnosed, of doctors.

The doctor went on to inform us that he had been coming to this place since before the war, indeed even under the Occupation life here had been bearable because Mr Štěrbák knew where to get hold of stuff and Mrs Štěrbáková knew how to prepare meals from virtually nothing, and when things had been really bad the Golden Stream had yielded the odd fish and the forest a few mushrooms or some blueberries for a cake. Besides, there was always something interesting going on. Next Sunday, for instance, there was a famous church fête in the nearby little town of Chlum and for that occasion the local amateur dramatic society was performing the unforgettable *Strakonice Bagpiper*. The doctor was convinced we would like it here and that we'd become regular habitués of the place, like the Havels for instance whom they'd met here a couple of years earlier and who were now spending their honeymoon here. The doctor pointed to the corner table, where a young couple were engaged in quiet conversation, and then he jerked his head towards a table by the window, where a featureless, pale, sickly-looking chap was sitting in solitary contemplation, a Mr Halama who'd been coming here for four years now and indeed sought refuge here occasionally when he needed peace and quiet. Dr Slavík chuckled significantly and I understood that some mystery attached to the pale man's presence.

Finally, to Mother's consternation, the doctor asked my father if by any chance he played *ferbl* or at least *liciťáček* because we could make up a splendid card party along with the schoolmaster Kalous, Mr Anton, Mr Sodomka from the railway and maybe also Mr Feuerstein from the fire brigade.

With a politeness that absolutely amazed me Father thanked him and said that unfortunately he'd brought along a lot of calculations he had to do because he was working on an exceptionally interesting solution of a three-phase commutator motor with core and he was afraid he wouldn't have much time left for amusements.

Mr Štěrbák meanwhile, still wearing his girlish apron, brought our schnitzels, and the doctor, having wished us *bon appetit*, returned to his table.

I could tell that my mother was irritated and disquieted not only by the importunate heartiness of the man but also by the knowledge that we were dining in a room which might at any moment be transformed into a gambling den.

She ate quickly and I was afraid that the moment we finished our schnitzels she would insist on leaving. Unlike her or my father, I would have liked to see how euchre or pontoon were played. I was also interested in the mysterious Mr Halama, the two newly-weds, the jovial doctor and, most of all, his companion.

After dinner, because this was a really hot day, my brother and I each got a bottle of yellowish lemonade, and my father made an exception and ordered a beer. Strange figures began to drift into the dining-room: the one that most captured my interest was a gaunt old man with milky hair and an unhealthy, red face. In contrast to everyone else in the room, with the exception of the doctor's wife, he was immaculately turned out in a dark suit. His neck stuck out of a high starched collar, of the kind my grandfather used to wear, and a fine gold chain hung from the pocket of his waistcoat which was an unusual, faintly lilac colour. Under his arm he carried a violin case. As he passed our table he bowed to my mother so that she, in her confusion, greeted him, to which he replied, 'I kiss your hand, gracious lady!' and immediately went on to bow to the doctor's wife and her husband. The doctor exclaimed, 'Excellent, my dear major-domo, what do you say to a game of cards after dinner?' And the old man replied, 'I am entirely at your service, doctor!'

At which point Mother nudged Father and rather loudly said, 'Shouldn't we be going?'

We took a walk along the river, the sun was already sinking behind the distant woods from a cloudless sky, a few late boats, quietly splashing, moved over the water and now and then a fish unexpectedly smacked against the surface.

Then we strolled down an avenue of tall poplars and limes, from which came the drawn-out wail of an accordion, and Mother reminded us how almost miraculous and unbelievable it was that we were walking together, all of us, and that we had survived the recent horrors and lived to see this moment. She urged us to watch how the sky was turning pink and red, how the sun dipped into the tops of indistinguishable trees, and asked if we knew or could picture anything more noble or perfect than this spectacle, and whether we could envisage a land more beautiful than our own.

Father smiled obediently and absently, his mind was probably on his three-phase commutator motor with core, and my brother declared that he was thirsty and that we should have brought along a pot to make some cocoa. It had not escaped him that, just before our departure, there had been a parcel from an aunt in Canada and that the parcel contained, among other things, a tin of that precious brown powder, and that Mother had slipped the tin into her case. The poor boy! No doubt, all the time he was supposed to be standing enthralled by nature's majesty he'd got all worked up by his vision of swallowing that divine beverage.

My mind, too, wandered for a while and I reflected that I'd be alone in my room at the inn in the evening and that I would be the absolute master of my time. The thought excited me.

The great master Maxim Gorky continued:

In each of them there lived, was tossed about, something dark and terrifying. The women squealed with pain as the men bit and pinched them, but they accepted such cruelty as necessary and even pleasurable, and Lyoska deliberately aroused Petrovsky with provocative shouts:

'More! Pinch me, go on!'

Her cat's eyes widened and she had the look at that moment of a female martyr in some painting. I was afraid Petrovsky might beat her to death . . . Now it seems to me that I saw enacted before me the heavy drama of conflict between two elements: bestiality and humanity. Man tries to assuage, once and for all, his bestial desire, to liberate himself from its insatiable longings, but it increases all the time and enslaves him more and more.

But soon these exuberant festivals of sensuous desire aroused revulsion and sadness in me, and at the same time I felt sorry for those people, especially the women. Although I tormented myself a lot, still I did not want to renounce participation in the madness of 'the monastic life'; or put more grandly, I was suffering from the fanaticism of knowledge, I was being destroyed and lured on by that 'fanatic of knowledge – Satan'.

From downstairs came a voice. The moment I heard it I identified the familiar alto laughter of my neighbour. What were they doing down there? What were they laughing at?

When she'd said goodnight to me Mother had specifically urged me to go straight to bed. She knew me, she said, and she realized that I wouldn't dream of loitering about in the bar downstairs. If only she'd forbidden me. The worst thing always is for someone to know something about a person and to trust him.

This was the first time in my life that I was spending a night in an inn. What was going to happen in this place? When would the other people go to their rooms? Would they do so at all or would they amuse themselves until daybreak? And what about those two newly-weds? What did newly-weds do together when they were alone? Surely they couldn't just do *that* all the time?

I shut my book and quietly stole to the window. It was night outside but, as the moon was nearly full, the darkness did not hide anything and the luminous river could be seen meandering through the grey landscape.

On the piece of meadow below the weir there were a number of tents, which must have been put up in the course of the evening. There was a small bonfire burning, a lot of dark figures were moving about, and I became aware of the faint sound of singing wafting over from there.

Surely they'd be together down there: boys and girls, men and women, pairs of lovers, they'd crawl into their tents together, they'd press themselves against each other, and then . . .

I ought at once to start reflecting on more serious

questions. What were more serious questions? The existence of God. Observation of life. The immortality of the human soul. Can Man be God and God Man? What is the nature of the human soul? What happens to the human soul at the epicentre of an atomic explosion? What is the meaning of life? War. What can I do against future wars? Or for my own immortality? Or for mankind? How do I attract love? Anyway, what is love? The books which I once . . .

In the next room a door creaked. I froze into immobility.

Barely audible footfalls. How many were there next door – one or two?

A few more quiet footsteps, a sigh – that surely was the alto sigh of the familiar female voice. If only these walls were transparent, if at least there was a tiny little crack in them.

As quietly as I could I slipped under my duvet and pressed my ear to the wall. It was cold and hard, and it seemed to me to be uttering its own stony whispers. The blood in its cold veins thumped with a loud ring in my ear. I didn't hear anything else; only when I'd put my head on my pillow did I hear the noisy creaking of a bed on the far side of the wall.

I froze in sweet anguish. It was as though the wall between us was about to dissolve. I dived under the duvet and waited motionless.

I was awakened by a trumpet. It sounded directly next to me. It gave me such a start that I leapt out from under my bedclothes and stared helplessly into the darkness. Then, as I slowly came to, I managed to locate the source of those metallic notes and I padded barefoot to the window.

Down there, under the chestnut-tree, stood a few moon-worshippers looking up at two players. One of the players, whom I easily recognized as Dr Slavík, was gripping a trumpet, while the other, judging by his white hair no doubt the extra-courteous Mr Anton, had a violin tucked under his chin. Together with those below I stared at the players and listened to the tune which, by the time it

31

reached me, had somehow managed to blend into the night, so that it seemed to carry the perfume of over-ripe blossoms and the warmth of the embraces of hidden lovers. It was so delightful that for a moment it separated the chilled soles of my feet from the rough floorboards and slipped beneath them like a gentle air cushion, and I was able to rock on its waves like a ship on a wind-tossed wave, or like a seagull on the edge of a stormcloud, and I could see the trumpet, raised upwards to the stars, gradually becoming engulfed in a golden flame that from below illuminated the chestnut-tree with its branches full of astonished birds.

Next to me a window creaked and, without being able to see that far, I sensed the proximity of a gentle female being, blowing kisses to the two musicians. At that moment I longed to be in their place, to be able to express my yearnings like that, to realize my visions. One day, perhaps, I would be able to do it, to compose words as perfectly as they composed their notes, and then I would call on some kindred soul, I'd find the love that would fill the whole of me.

The tune came to an end, the trumpet was extinguished, the branches of the chestnut-tree were plunged back into darkness and I dropped back on to the floorboards. But as I was backing towards my bed I caught a glimpse of the two musicians bowing to the invisible lady; a moment later they were swallowed up by the clump of moon-worshippers who joyfully carried them off into the darkness, presumably to plant them under some other, more distant, window.

The next day I awoke much too early. For a while I tossed and turned on my bed in the hope of hearing something interesting. Then I felt ashamed at the way I was wasting my time.

I stepped out of my room at the precise moment when the door opposite opened, revealing a tousled female head. I recognized young Mrs Havel. She was wearing a floral dressing-gown and carrying two vases of wild poppies and cornflowers.

I blushed as if she had caught me in some improper pursuit and stammered good morning.

She smiled at me with her large, pale mouth, clutched the glass containers to her bosom and said she was off to change the water for the flowers.

Inside her room I caught sight of several more vases filled with wild flowers. Maybe that was part of being in love or being newly wed, but then the door was shut from inside.

We walked down the stairs together. To keep silent seemed rather rude to me, so I asked, 'Do you pick them yourself?'

'With my husband,' she said, uttering the word proudly. 'We're both fond of flowers.'

The pump was in the courtyard and I offered to help her. I caught hold of the pump-handle.

'I recently dreamt of a marvellous flower,' she said. 'It was shaped like a bell and was flame-coloured, but with a dark-blue receptacle. And it was almost as large as a water-lily.'

'Maybe you'll find one like that,' I burst out.

'That would be wonderful,' she breathed. 'I can picture it as I walk across the meadow. But it probably grows somewhere in the tropics.'

She picked up the vases again in her thin hands. 'If you like I can pick some for you,' she said and turned towards the stairs while I made for Mr Pavelec's farm.

I found my parents in the middle of a heated argument. During the night, it seemed, there had been a mouse in their room and, what's more, my mother had learned from Mrs Pavelec that her brother, a Mr Valeš who lived in the building next door, had TB. Mother was always a stickler for cleanliness – of body, soul and surroundings. The idea of breathing air into which, just round the corner, someone was coughing the life-destroying germs of tuberculosis terrified her. She demanded of my father that we should instantly pack our cases and leave.

Father clearly did not want to. He was glad to have found a bed and a table on which he could spread his papers, charts and slide-rule. Except that in situations like this nobody gave a damn about Father's interests.

It looked as if removal was inevitable when Father in his despair suddenly remembered our dining-room neighbour and proposed that he should ask him whether the occurrence of disease in the house next door could threaten any of us.

Although Mother objected angrily that she had no faith in doctors anyway, Father, now that he had conceived his possible solution, would not be deflected.

Dr Slavík was clearly pleased. He immediately pulled a chair over to our table and assured my mother that it would be difficult to find a healthier spot than Mr Pavelec's farm. As for the Koch bacilli, those were present everywhere, and everything really came down to how a person managed to coexist with them. He then began to talk about Mr Valeš. Poor chap, a victim of the war, indeed of his own gallantry, but also – no denying it – of his ambition. Frank Valeš, the doctor related, used to be a keen gymnast, a healthy and well-built chap, a musician and a cross-country runner. Later on he mainly chased skirts with even more success in that field.

Just then the cadaverous Mr Halama entered the dining-room. As he passed our table he said, 'Good morning, everyone!' and it struck me that this carefully enunciated greeting sounded false or perhaps over-rehearsed. In the morning his features were even pastier and his eyes were a muddy grey. He sat down mournfully at the table by the window. He noticed that I was watching him and immediately turned away. His glance and his movements betrayed the unease of the outcast.

Just before the war – the doctor meanwhile continued his story – Frank had got married, to one Mařenka Sodomková, a local beauty and the star of the Tyl amateur dramatic ensemble. Thereupon he founded a band which played at club dances, funerals, weddings and other festivities. Mařenka at first did not like Frank gadding about in the evenings, but soon she began to realize that it was only when she was at home by herself that she got a proper night's sleep. Here the doctor chuckled meaningly, Mother pretended to be shocked, Father was far away (probably solving some difficult technical problem in his mind) and the doctor's fair-haired wife provocatively crossed a suntanned leg over a suntanned knee and emitted cloudlets of smoke into the sunlit air.

The band had soon made a name for itself and got engagements throughout the neighbourhood. The Germans left them alone because they played brass-band music by Kmoch and fishermen's ditties such as 'Annie's walking down the lane with a huge carp that she has slain' or 'My father was a fisherman and sailed the stormy sea'. The people went for that kind of music, and the doctor could make a long story of it because on his holidays they sometimes allowed him to join them with his trumpet. Except that one day in Chlum, that was in forty-four, old Hamerník died (he was the chairman of the Hradec Králové regional branch of the national gymnastic organization, Sokol, and had personally known Tyrš, founder of the gymnasts' association, and had taken part in all ten Sokol Congresses), and so members had gathered from far and wide, and four bands had turned up for the funeral. And on that occasion Frank not only played 'With lion's strength' but also that marvellous solemn bit from Smetana's 'Má Vlast', or more precisely from 'Tábor', which he had personally arranged and rehearsed for the funeral. And when he came to the Hussite hymn – and here the doctor stood up and sang: 'That in the end Victory shall be yours' – someone suddenly started to sing and a moment later the ancient battle hymn rang throughout the cemetery, just as if the Hussite armies were really marching to the rescue. The Germans, of course, couldn't fail to hear the singing, and they picked up the man who started it all, even before he got back home, and kept him at Gestapo headquarters in Budějovice for two months.

Mr Halama was served his morning coffee, he sipped it slowly, and it seemed to me that he would have liked to bury his face in his hands. That man was hiding from something: with his fair hair, his grey eyes and his over-careful pronunciation who knows if he weren't a German? There were a lot of them around, it was said. They'd got hold of false papers and now they were living amongst us and nobody could guess what they might have on their consciences or what they might be plotting.

When Frank got back, the doctor continued, there was scarcely half of him left. His teeth had been knocked out, his hands were shaking, his mind was traumatized and he had Koch's bacillus in his lungs. True, after the war they repaired his teeth and sent him to a sanatorium, but he signed a slip of paper and ran away to find his Mařenka. Simply because, faced with the decision of dying in bed on his own or with a woman, he chose the latter and, indeed, was well on the way to that end.

My mother acted as if she were carved from a block of ice. She urged Father for heaven's sake not to delay the doctor any longer, and a moment later she rose, and we went down to the river.

Neither Mother nor I went in. My mother didn't because years before a famous cardiologist had told her that her heart was so exceptionally and remarkably delicate that even the slightest exertion could kill her. Admittedly it turned out later that this wrong diagnosis was due to the fact that Mother's cardiogram had been mixed up with the cardiogram of some elderly woman who was actually dying, so that Mother's heart in fact was quite normal and sound, but for safety's sake my mother continued to avoid all exertion.

I didn't go in because contact with the wet element gave me no pleasure. What reconciled me to being by the river was the large number of females around. They ran about or lay on the

36

ground exposing their beautiful and desirable bodies to the sun and to my gaze. I pretended to be reading but I was watching the newly-wed Havels lying, closely pressed together, on a strip of an only partially opened blanket, and the doctor's wife and her daughters who were throwing a ball to each other.

My father and brother came out of the water. My brother remembered the cocoa in Mother's suitcase and proposed that we should go to the forest, light a fire and prepare some hot drink. Meanwhile, still pretending to read, I had noticed that some of the bathers, when they wanted to change out of their wet things, ran across the foot-bridge with their clothes and beach-bags and disappeared on the far side of the island. Mother snapped at my brother not to think of his stomach all the time and set me up as an example: I hadn't even been in the water yet but, poor chap, constantly had my nose in my books. Father sided with my brother and remarked that a little exercise wouldn't do me any harm either. With a thought suddenly taking shape inside me, I announced that I would go for a walk in the afternoon.

As soon as lunch was over, I was off, in the scorching heat of the sun, to the far side of the river.

I found a spot in the tall grass. When I lay down I couldn't be seen from the island, whereas I could see everything.

I was feeling ashamed of my action, at the base and contemptible nature of my motives, although for a while I tried to pretend to myself that I had chosen that spot because of its particular isolation so that I might read and reflect undisturbed. I did actually lie on my back and watch a few lonely clouds hanging almost motionless above my head. It was a calming and exalting feeling to be looking up. I thought of my friends, of boys my own age who were no longer able to gaze at the sky like this because they were dead, poisoned by gas. Were they at least looking down from above? Can the human soul see?

I doubted it, I doubted the immortality of the human soul, or, more accurately, I couldn't picture it. The form in which it might continue to exist, or the space in which it might do so. Even though the universe was vast enough to contain any number of souls. Except that in interstellar space there was, apparently, such cold that anything alive would instantly freeze into immobility.

I was so captivated by the idea that I opened the book into which I had placed a sheet of paper, just in case, and with a pencil stub noted down:

At best the human soul has a choice between the heat of hell and the iciness of heaven.

Then something else occurred to me:

It is therefore better to believe in the immortality of love than in the immortality of the soul!

For a while I gazed at those two sentences in blissful amazement. They sounded as if they had been thought up by a real writer. I therefore added the date and folded the paper back into my book.

One day, when I was famous as an educated, interesting, witty and honoured artist, I wouldn't need to lie concealed on a river bank under a swarm of midges; I should be sitting in my study, or strolling out through my front door and they would come running up to me of their own accord. Not only ordinary, uninteresting women but maybe even famous actresses. I was visualizing myself dining in a night-club with a famous actress, touching her exquisite naked arms, when suddenly two strange girls appeared over the crest of the island, in swimsuits and with large bags.

My heart started thumping. Just then a waterbird flew up from the reeds close to me. As I looked angrily in that direction I caught sight of the pale, glum and mysterious Mr Halama shuffling along the narrow path which at that point came down nearly to water level.

Those two had obviously seen him and while he, without taking any notice of them, was moving away along the river, they disappeared into a thicket on that side of the island and were totally lost from sight.

I was lying motionless in my grassy hideout. Now and again I seemed to catch a flicker of a girl's body in the opaque tangle of branches and leaves, but I could not be sure.

When they re-emerged they were wearing colourful little dresses, calling out to each other and quickly climbing towards the low ridge of the island; a moment later they had disappeared. Mr Halama too had vanished in the distance. Where had he gone? I would have said that path led somewhere to the railway line or perhaps straight to the station.

For a moment I toyed with the idea that Mr Halama, who wasn't called Halama at all but Heindel or Hoes, was off to some top secret meeting with an emissary of the condemned, but still untraced, Martin Bormann. He was hiding out – after all, who'd be looking for him there – in the frontier forests between the Treestump, the Hare and the Three Slaps mountains. And I would be the one to discover him, or at least to discover his hideout.

As I returned to my little room before dinner the door next to mine opened and the tanned face of the doctor's wife looked out. 'Oh, it's you,' she said. 'I thought it might be my husband. You haven't seen him anywhere, have you?'

'I'm afraid not.' It seemed to me that the fragrance of lilies-of-the-valley was wafting through the half-open door of her room. 'I thought he'd gone fishing.'

'God knows where he's knocking about! And what about you – I didn't see you by the river this afternoon?'

'I went for a walk.'

'And how far did you go?' She fixed her pale-blue eyes on me and I could feel myself blushing.

'I was just strolling along the bank. And then I read for a while.'

39

'You probably read a lot,' the doctor's wife flicked her head so that her fair hair flew up around her head. She leaned her shoulder against the door frame and pointed to the book in my hand.

'Only during vacations!' In my excitement I half-opened the book so that the sheet with my text slipped out and floated to her feet.

She bent down quickly, before I managed to do so, picked up the paper and handed it to me. Fortunately the sheet was folded with the writing inside, only today's date was peeping out. 'Oh that's just something I jotted down,' I felt a need to justify the sheet of paper and again I blushed.

'I used to be fond of reading, too!' She pretended not to notice my embarrassment. 'When I was a lot younger. *The Forests Sang Forever, North against South, When the Rains Came* . . . I would read books and think Heaven knew what I would encounter in my life. But it's all a big con. Lots of beautiful words about love, about faithfulness and imagined incidents. And you just walk along the river, that's all?'

I nodded.

'I wonder! You've probably got a girl down there from one of those tents, while your own girl is faithfully waiting somewhere for a letter from you.' She laughed with that alto voice of hers, threatened me with her suntanned forefinger and, without waiting for me to refute those frightful and unsubstantiated accusations, said, 'I know what you're like, you men!'

Just then some shouting came from below, 'Everybody come and look!' and I recognized her husband's voice.

We both went downstairs. In the kitchen doorway stood the doctor, in waders with a rod by his side and a huge bulging creel, yelling at Mrs Štěrbáková to bring her largest dish or, better still, a washtub.

Mrs Štěrbáková appeared, pushing rather than carrying a huge earthenware pot. Dr Slavík opened his waterproof creel and began to chuck out from it the slithery bodies of fish, with expressions of noisy delight: 'Some whoppers, what?' Then he turned to Mrs Štěrbáková and recited:

> 'If we are taught that pot
> Comes from the verb to pit,
> Then what's the origin of shot?
> Or can't you answer it?'

'Doctor, doctor,' the innkeeper's wife was well-rounded, pink-cheeked and good-natured, 'where on earth do you get these dreadful poems from?'

'From my patients, Mrs Štěrbáková!' said Dr Slavík, who, with his sleeves rolled up, was fishing more fish out of his creel. 'And do you know this one?' He began to sing:

> 'I don't like women who are short,
> They've got it too close to the ground
> And when they walk down muddy streets
> It gets all splashed, I've always found.'

He flung the last fish into the earthenware pot, the innkeeper's wife laughed happily, while the doctor's wife looked at me as if to say: Don't be annoyed, I've long stopped being annoyed, that's the kind of life I've got! But I was glad my mother wasn't present. If she had heard all those improper verses we'd be packing our bags that very day.

Mother didn't appear for dinner either, it seemed she had a headache from the sun, so only my father and my brother came.

The dining-room by then was full: in addition to the mysterious and solitary Mr Halama, and Mr Anton in his old-world attire, there were two men sitting there in uniform, one of them evidently a railwayman and the other apparently a fireman. At the table by the window a little man was reading *Rudé Právo*; all I could see of him was a grey tuft of hair, black trouser-legs, and of course the fingers holding his paper. From them, or maybe because of my

41

irrepressible longing for education, I guessed that the man behind the paper might be Kalous, the schoolmaster.

From the kitchen came the smell of sizzling fat, in which the doctor's carp were being fried, and a moment later the doctor himself appeared in the doorway, in light-coloured trousers and white canvas shoes. His wife, too, had changed, into a red striped dress with a plunging neckline on which, directly in the cleavage between her breasts, she had pinned a honey-yellow artificial rose which, I noticed, trembled with delight at every inhalation and exhalation of its wearer.

The doctor looked around, and when he caught sight of the guests he let out a joyful whoop: 'Why, look who's visiting us! The schoolmaster along with . . . Mrs Štěrbáková, get a jug of water ready just in case the place catches fire – along with Mr Feuerstein! *Nomen est omen*, I always say. And just as everyone realizes the moment I introduce myself – Slavík meaning nightingale – that I'm a useful singer, and just as the schoolmaster won't deny that he is a somewhat morose sage, so everyone looking at you, Mr Feuerstein, and hearing your name, must realize that you are that little flint that scatters sparks among barns and hayricks!'

Only then did I study the little man in the fireman's uniform. I noticed his hair, which really was the colour of flames; his small eyes looked shifty to me and his large prominent ears struck me as those of a criminal.

Strangely enough, Mr Feuerstein did not mind those accusations. He even laughed and remarked that only two days before they'd put out a fire in a rick just beyond Chlum; the wisps of burning straw had soared higher than the top of the local church spire. The man in railwayman's uniform added that they'd received a special circular on the railways to the effect that the exceptional drought meant an increased danger of forest and crop fires, and that the tracks should be continually patrolled to make sure some spark from an engine hadn't started a fire. And, in fact, one guard together with a man from dispatch had set out along the track towards Lomnice – of course they didn't have any apparatus with them, not even a water bucket, or so much as a beer mug – and just where the track swung away from the pond they spotted some grass burning. At first, they broke off some branches to beat out the flames, but the fire had already got too much of a hold, so the guard took off his tunic and tried to smother the flames with it, only the tunic soon caught fire and they had to chuck it on the ground and stamp on it, but as they were jumping on it their trousers and the soles of their shoes began to smoke so that in the end they had to run to Lomnice to call out the fire brigade. They didn't return to the station till late at night and they were all singed. 'I made a painting of them the moment they got back,' the man in the blue uniform announced.

We were all listening attentively; only Mr Halama, I noticed, was sitting unconcerned at his table, staring out of the window towards the river.

I should have liked to ask what happened about the conflagration but Mrs Štěrbáková was coming round just then with the plates and announced in a loud voice that, thanks to the doctor here, tonight's dinner was off ration cards and only the side dishes would be charged for. At these words the doctor rose to his feet and bowed to everybody. He then asked the man in the railwayman's uniform, whom he addressed as Mr Sodomka, if he'd brought that picture with him. The railwayman immediately opened a long leather case and obligingly produced a roll of canvas. When he'd unrolled it we saw a painting of two men in blue uniforms which were singed all over. Steam was rising from the big skulls of the two railwaymen, starting off faintly pink, as if from flames, but as it rose upwards the smoke turned blue until finally it was almost white, and in that white shape it wafted through two laurel wreaths which hung in a clear, blue sky.

'Now that's a real masterpiece you have there,' Dr Slavík commended the picture. 'You've really immortalized those two heroes, Mr Sodomka. Have you brought us anything else?'

Mr Sodomka immediately produced another little roll of canvas, and, even though the innkeeper's wife was just placing his plate before him, he unrolled the canvas and held it so that we could all see. The picture represented a meadow in the moonlight. In the meadow a silvery brown deer with a black dog-like snout was grazing, about to be shot by a huntsman. The doctor was delighted that, for the second time that day, he had an opportunity to recite his doggerel about the shot and the pot. When he'd finished his recital everybody laughed, except the doctor's wife. I looked at her and she at me, and a fleeting smile appeared on her round suntanned face, but that smile really belonged to me and I realized that she was saying to me: Now you can see for yourself! I'd expected so much from life and all I'm getting is lubricious doggerel.

I cut myself a piece of carp – I was not particularly fond of fish but this one tasted different from any fish I'd ever had – and as I was chewing that first mouthful a strange exhilaration gripped me. Life seemed to me good, interesting and even exciting: a marvellous life in which things were happening, and those happenings were surrounding me, lifting me up, as air might surround and lift up a balloon rising above the earth.

After dinner the doctor grandly addressed his wife 'My love!' and asked her if she would have any objections to his indulging in a game of cards. The lady replied that he'd have his game anyway, even if she did object, so why didn't he just do what he liked. She rose at once, motioned to the twins, and left the dining-room with them. Thereupon Mr Štěrbák went over to their table, removed the cloth and placed some paper beermats and a pack of cards on the bare wooden top. A moment later the places which had been occupied by the doctor's family were taken by Mr Kalous, the schoolmaster, Mr Feuerstein, the fireman, and Mr Sodomka, the railway-man-painter. He announced that he would only kibitz.

Dr Slavík pulled the cards out of the packet, said that the lowest card deals, and cut.

There was no card-playing in our home, just as there was no bad language, no drinking and not even smoking. I expected my father to get up at once and to order us out, but instead he pulled his chair up closer to the doctor's table so he could watch better.

By now there were stacks of banknotes and piles of small change lying on the table and Mr Feuerstein exclaimed that he had a seven, whereupon the doctor announced that he'd risk a hundred and what's more a hundred in hearts. And when the teacher replied: A hundred in trumps, let him play it then but he'd like to see him do it, the doctor picked up the last two cards which were lying forgotten on the table and declared *misère*.

Slam, slam, and the doctor showed everyone his cards, swept up three ten-crown notes and, in order to cheer the others up, declared, 'First winning, disaster's beginning,' and washed down his proverb with a mighty gulp of beer.

I didn't understand anything. One moment they were playing, the next moment one player simply showed his cards and immediately swept up his winnings – but, nevertheless, I watched closely the movement of the cards and the money. I sided with the doctor against the schoolmaster but the schoolmaster kept winning because, as I gathered from the doctor's remarks, not only was God not at home but Mr Feuerstein was also continually making mistakes.

'And why did you have to play leaves,' the doctor screamed at him, 'when they're your weakest suit?'

'I thought I would undercut his ten,' the man in the fireman's uniform defended himself, while the school-master was raking up a fistful of coins.

'For Christ's sake,' the doctor grumbled, 'when you're back home, Mr Feuerstein, you get out your fireman's tomahawk and chop off that nut of yours so you won't think so much!'

45

And so it went on. I was practically in despair as I watched the grey hundred-crown notes piling up in front of the schoolmaster. I noticed that whenever he drew some notes towards him his thin lips trembled imperceptibly in a self-satisfied smirk. No doubt that was how he smirked when, hands folded behind his back, he dictated to the poor devils in his class: Construct a regular quadrilateral whose diagonals intersect at right angles . . . Just then the schoolmaster somewhat nervously bid a hundred in acorns, and from the expression on the doctor's face I realized that the turning point in the game had arrived at last. He smacked his cards making a noise like a gunshot and exclaimed: 'Double to you, schoolmaster, and saddle your steed for your hour of need!'

Except that once again Mr Feuerstein didn't come up to expectations. The schoolmaster swept up a fistful of ten-crown notes and the doctor asked despairingly: 'Mr Feuerstein, why didn't you pull out your ace of leaves when you saw that the last train was leaving? Saving it up for next Christmas or something?'

'It seemed to me . . . ' the red-haired fireman stuttered.

'To seem is to dream,' yelled the doctor. 'When you get home you take that tomahawk of yours and knock your forehead with it to wake you up a little before going to bed.'

In the next hand, when the schoolmaster announced that 'Seven bells is what my hand tells,' Mr Feuerstein, perhaps to redeem himself, declared 'Double!' in a loud voice and a moment later 'And treble!' which cost him and his partner a cool twenty-four crowns. The red-haired fireman heaved a silent sigh, what's done is done, but the doctor groaned in despair that Mr Feuerstein must be in love, and intoned:

> 'A pussy that dropped from the sky
> On a fireman caused him to cry:
> I'm covered with hair
> But I'm nearly there,
> Though my balls are caught up in my fly.'

And I, even though I still didn't understand any of the drama unrolling before me, was enthralled by the game, almost breathless with excitement. When the cards were dealt again I could sense the hopes rising in the hot air of the dining-room and, at that moment, I forgot everything that would normally have filled my mind – my plans, my mission, the works of the great masters, my mother, my father and my brother, and even the doctor's beautiful wife who no doubt was lying on her bed beyond the wall of my little room – and it seemed to me that we must all be bewitched in the same way. But then I was roused by an inappropriate noise from the corner of the room: I cast a quick glance in that direction and saw the newly-wed Havels, apparently oblivious to what was happening, getting up from their chairs. As they approached the doctor's table she looked at the players and with amazement, or perhaps even compassion, covered her face with a bunch of whitish-yellow marguerites. Her new husband tenderly caught hold of her, slipped his flat hand under her buttock and gently lifted her, until he was holding her above the table-top and above our heads, and walked slowly between us, while she, from her elevated position behind the white wild-flower petals, gave us a tender and absent-minded smile with her pale lips which were chapped either from the heat or from kisses.

At that precise moment, as the two newly-weds were pushing through the tall doorway, it happened.

The schoolmaster bid a seven of hearts, backed by a seven of bells. And while he was still making his bid, without waiting for his opponents' reply, he stretched his cruel lips in a victorious smirk. But the doctor merely shot a rapid glance at his hand and uttered almost hesitantly: 'Schoolmaster, I'll double both your sevens!'

For a moment the schoolmaster looked at him in astonishment. Then he asked: 'Are you sure you've added up correctly, doctor?'

'Never been so sure in my life,' the doctor replied almost

in a whisper and he seemed to be trembling with anxiety. 'You saddle your steed for your hour of need!'

'The higher one, then, doctor!' said the schoolmaster. 'Because I've got it all here, I can show you my hand!'

'You can do that,' the doctor said happily, now quite loudly. 'But first let me give you a double, and don't you wriggle any more. Because, when you show us your hand you'll be looking in vain for that seven of hearts, which happens to have been dealt to me!'

And I could see the schoolmaster turning pale. His thin lips almost disappeared into his face and he whispered: 'My God, what an idiot I am!'

'You're that, all right,' the doctor could not restrain himself; 'you shout from the rooftops that you have the higher seven and in actual fact you have bugger-all!'

The schoolmaster turned even paler and in a pinched voice asked: 'What are you suggesting, doctor?'

'You heard me,' the doctor now expounded to the whole room. 'You undertake to play what you haven't got and simply rely on others not to notice it. Except that we here,' he pointed at Mr Feuerstein, 'aren't taken in by fine words, we're old hands at cards!' And the red-haired fireman was beaming quietly and told the schoolmaster not to be angry, that what was bound to happen had happened.

The schoolmaster, however, rose to his feet and, in a voice so sharp that it cut, declared: 'That, doctor, I won't take from you!'

'Well, well, well,' the doctor expressed surprise. 'I haven't said anything offensive, have I?'

'Everything you say,' the schoolmaster declared, 'is offensive. You practically spew swinish filth. You should at least feel some shame in front of those young people,' he jerked his head in the direction of our table. 'But as you see fit to . . . Only I won't stand for your digs at my convictions. We don't try to take anybody in with fine words,' the schoolmaster continued, raising his voice more and more, 'we merely demand that the people should receive what has long been their due. The fruits of their labour, a fair wage and a share in the government. And liberation from those who have to this day exploited them with impunity. And you, you should pull yourself together and find your proper place before it's too late. How much do I owe you, gentlemen?'

I noticed that the schoolmaster's speech had appealed to my father and that he only just managed to restrain himself from saying something about the people's right to a better future, while everyone else was staring at the schoolmaster with something like consternation as he calmly counted up all the hundred-crown notes on the table in front of him, added another three from his wallet, divided the notes into two piles and with a powerful movement of his hand brushed them towards the centre of the table.

'But, schoolmaster . . . ' the red-haired fireman said in alarm.

Except that the schoolmaster took no notice of him. He rose and into the empty space he found between our heads said icily: 'Good night, gentlemen!' And he walked out of the dining-room as coolly as if he were leaving a classroom where he had just entered everybody's name in the punishment book.

'First you with the Devil sit,' the doctor commented on the schoolmaster's abrupt departure, 'then he drops you in the shit!'

The great master Stendhal wrote:

Madame de Renal was frightened to death by Julian's arrival; she was gripped by terror. His tears and his despair unbalanced her. Even when she no longer had anything to deny him she would push Julian away with real indignation, though a moment later she would fling herself into his arms. She was acting like a person bereft of her senses. She was convinced that she was mercilessly condemned to eternal perdition and she endeavoured to drown her thoughts of hell in the most passionate kisses. Nothing would have been wanting in Julian's happiness, not

49

*even the ardent emotions of the woman who had just given
herself to him, if he had been able to take pleasure from it. . . .
'Good Lord! To be happy, to be loved, is just this?' was Julian's
first thought as he returned to his room.*

The next morning when I looked out of the window, I saw
to my amazement the red-haired Mr Feuerstein sitting on a
branch of the chestnut-tree. Even before I could discover
what he was doing there he spotted me and waved with
some object I couldn't identify, but it could have been the
tomahawk that had been mentioned, and, as I wasn't sure
whether his gesture was friendly or threatening, I thought it
wiser to retreat from the window. By the time I'd screwed
up my courage, the red-haired fireman was no longer up the
tree; however, hanging from the branches were strange and
colourful bits of string, or possibly wire, whose purpose I
didn't understand.

I didn't find any of our new friends by the river. I
pretended to myself that that the one I was missing most
was the doctor. If I joined him in the morning I would be
sure to learn a lot of interesting things or at least some
amusing anecdotes. What I really minded was that his wife
wasn't there – and that consequently my eyes had nothing
to feast on.

Even before elevenses (my mother had shoved a roll into
my pocket, beautifully wrapped in a paper napkin) I left the
river again.

In the field nearby a half-naked farmer with a single horse
harnessed to his plough was turning the soil. Behind the
furrow rose a tall, almost transparent, pillar of dust. A grey
haze was hanging above the whole parched plain and the
air above the ground was quivering and vibrating.

The village yawned with emptiness; even the dogs had
crept wearily into their kennels and did not pay me their
usual attention.

I stopped in front of the village shop and gazed at the
colourful enamelled sign which advertised in crimson

Velim chicory, in azure Oettker's baking powder and in red-and-white Helada soap. Or else they glorified detergents in verse:

> OTAMYR drives out all dirt,
> Leaves you with a snow-white shirt!

Mr Anton came out of the door. He was not carrying his violin, but in the midday heat he was dressed like the leader of an orchestra in a black suit with waistcoat, and with an old-fashioned bowler hat hiding his white hair.

I said good morning to him and he raised his hat and inquired where I was bound for.

I wasn't bound for anywhere, whereas he was on his way to the cemetery and suggested that I might accompany him.

I was afraid of cemeteries. Certainly not because of any ghosts but because they reminded me too much of my ephemeral existence. But I was too ashamed to turn the old man down and so I set out with him along the dusty track.

He asked where I was at school, where I lived and how old I was, and then he said that when he was my age he'd already left for Vienna, where he had a job as a junior waiter in the famous Kirschner restaurant.

'That would have still been under the Emperor?'

'That was sixty-four years ago,' he said with precision. 'In those days I didn't know too much about His Majesty. But when I was taken on by His Highness, our Prince, as a major-domo I had the honour to see His Majesty from quite close to. On three occasions. Once I served him a glass of wine at a banquet. Another time I was permitted to attend a hunting party in which His Majesty was personally participating.'

I had had no idea about Mr Anton's strange occupation. Until then I'd only known major-domos from novels. 'And did you shoot anything yourself?' I asked.

'The quality would shoot,' he explained. 'We saw to it that they had good refreshments the moment they returned from hunting.'

'But that wasn't fair,' I objected, remembering what I'd heard about equality, liberty and fraternity.

'Which of us knows what is fair?'

By then I could see, beyond the strip of yellowish meadow, a low wall with a few crosses showing above it.

'People are contemptuous of anyone who is not ashamed to serve another,' Mr Anton said. 'But which of them does not serve? Even the gentlemen who rule serve somebody. I've always maintained that a man can do anything so long as he does it lovingly. Without love there's no contentment. And it is according to the degrees of love that one day the one supreme justice will sort us out. Understand what I'm saying?'

I nodded. We had reached the cemetery. The old man opened the black-painted iron gate and we entered.

'The third time I saw His Majesty was a very sorrowful occasion – the funeral of Her Majesty. On the sixteenth of September it was, six days after that rascal Lucheni treacherously stabbed her in the chest.'

Needless to say I had never heard of the event.

'On that occasion I saw many rulers,' Mr Anton added. 'Their Majesties the Emperor Wilhelm, King Alexander of Serbia and the Archduke Alexis of Russia. All those carriages, outriders and teams of six black horses. Black flags flying from all the windows.'

It was a small cemetery, only three rows of graves. At the far wall a huge lime-tree shaded the low building of the burial chapel; in the window of a little tower hung the motionless dark mass of a bell.

On my right, next to the entrance, I saw a well with a pump, and by the pump stood a watering can. Mr Anton filled it with water, I took the can from him and he led me to a grave with a grey limestone cross; on it I read: Anna Antonová 1871–1908.

Under the name and date I could make out a faded quatrain:

> The Lord hath measured out thy life
> And put an end upon thine earthly tide.
> Now slumber softly, my dear wife,
> Until the Lord shall raise you to His side.

Mr Anton spoke the words of some prayer in a half-voice. I moved away a little distance so as not to disturb him.

The lime was in full flower, the other graves too had blossoms and the air was heavy with a sweet blend of perfumes.

'I have never forgotten you,' whispered Mr Anton, bowing his milky white head low towards the cemetery wall, 'and He knows that. He will grant our souls to meet again forever in His Kingdom of love.'

I was ashamed to be hearing something that wasn't intended for me, and moved away further still, until my back was against the hot brick wall. From the crown of the lime-tree came the buzz of bees and the cooing of a wood pigeon.

I looked at the gravestones and crosses in front of me and to my surprise I felt no fear. Indeed a tranquillity came over me as though I were already waist-deep in the ground, as though an angel were already spreading his wings above me.

And I noticed that a small, reddish pigeon flew out of the tree-top, circled over us, and then landed by the old man's side, hopped up to his hat, extended its neck over the black brim and dipped its beak into it and drank. I could see quite clearly the gleaming surface of the water with which that old hat was filled, and I watched other birds gliding down to us on quiet wings to refresh themselves.

The old man crossed himself, rose to his feet, crossed himself again, then, with a slow movement of his elderly hand, blessed the drinking birds, picked up the hat from the ground and said to me: 'So you see that the same measure of this hallowed ground is enough for all of us. And I have outlived them all.'

He gazed into the distance after the departing birds and, in a flash of illumination, I realized whom he was talking about, that the souls of all the rulers, emperors, kings and princes he had ever seen, and whom he had perhaps served well and with love, and whom he had survived, had just flown here to meet him.

In the afternoon, as I was strolling towards Mr Pavelec's farm, a familiar voice – what bliss – called out to me and when I turned I saw the doctor's wife, radiant as ever. She caught up with me and said that her husband had sent her to take some medicine to Mr Valeš, whose condition had deteriorated over the past few days.

We were therefore going the same way and the deliciously smelling lady declared that she was pleased, as she didn't like walking on her own.

Boldly I said that I didn't like walking on my own either.

'I've been wondering about you,' she remarked; 'a young man like you and still travelling with your mother. Wouldn't you rather go somewhere with your girl?'

I blushed and said that I didn't have a girl just then.

'Come, come, what about that letter yesterday? It's not nice to deny one's love!'

She shook her finger at me, laughed and said not to worry, she wouldn't give me away. After all, why shouldn't a young chap like me have a girl friend? It was worse when married men chased girls – she could tell a tale or two about that because the worst men of all in that respect were doctors.

The smile had gone from her face and I suspected that she'd picked this subject only as a pretext for confiding her own sufferings to me. I would have liked to convince her that I wasn't denying anyone, that I had never denied anyone or betrayed anyone, and indeed would not be capable of any such action, but she was talking all the time. She had never wanted to believe that the world was full of deceit and betrayal, she had been foolish, a dreamer, she'd often spent her nights picturing to herself what her man would be like, and perhaps she'd even met such a one. A classmate of hers, a gentle and sensitive man, with large, brown, childlike eyes, just like mine. He'd asked her out to the park a few times and once she'd gone dancing with him. On her way home, and she'd never forget that evening, they had seen a big fire in the distance. A grain store was ablaze, and that conflagration seemed to presage a far bigger conflagration, because a few days later the Germans came and the war started. Someone had evidently seen her at that dance and denounced her to her father, because her father had started a frightful fireworks so that it all ended before it could even begin. 'And so a person misses his or her only love,' she said sadly and wisely, 'and often doesn't even realize it. Which is perhaps just as well because, if he realized it, he'd take a few tablets to go to sleep, and never wake up again.' And a tear welled from the heavenly eyes of the doctor's wife and descended in a moist trickle down her suntanned face.

On the wall of Mr Valeš's farm was a slightly faded inscription: VOTE LIST 3.

The doctor's wife pulled a handkerchief from her handbag, wiped her eyes and said: 'Like this poor chap, he'll soon have it all behind him!' And she added that he used to be a lot of fun and was never a spoilsport, but now she was almost afraid to go in. But what else could she do? He was all alone almost the whole day, lying there with his illness, just wasting away. She'd try and cheer him up a bit; if I liked I could wait for her, she couldn't bear it in there for long anyway. Then she disappeared in the door and I sat down obediently on a shady, low wall under the open window.

I was experiencing a strange excitement but also some anguish from the knowledge that there behind that wall was a desperately sick person, that behind that wall death was already lurking, and suppose its eye fell on me too? At this thought I was overcome by anxiety and I would probably have got up and left immediately had I not heard the doctor's wife's charming deep voice in the house.

'Everything will be all right again, Frankie!' she was saying. 'You'll be waiting for me again at our spot in the woods.'

'Not any more,' a strange male voice replied. 'I wouldn't even get that far now.'

'I've brought you some new medicine,' the doctor's wife said, 'some Swiss stuff!'

'No medicine can give me back my lungs!' The man began to cough. 'What about your husband, does he still play the trumpet?'

'Don't talk,' the doctor's wife asked him. 'You see how it exhausts you. Better save your strength!' A strange light radiated from her hair, illuminating the room all the way to me outside, and I understood that those two people were bound together by some ancient secret.

'It doesn't matter now,' the man objected; 'nothing matters now. At least here. And over there you don't need any strength.'

'You mustn't think about that.'

'But I do. If there is any over there. Another reunion with those one's been fond of.'

'Of course there is,' I heard the doctor's wife say. 'We'll all meet there one day, but you aren't to think of that just yet!'

'Our reverend's been here to see me, he said the same thing. But I don't know. They're all just trying to comfort me.'

'Wait, I'll get some water for you,' the doctor's wife changed the subject, 'then you can swallow your tablets. Supposed to be some wonder drug. You'll see, you'll soon be running about again.'

'Not me, my lungs are gone. And don't give me any tablets. It's not worth it. Do you think your husband will play for me?'

'Now that's enough,' the doctor's wife almost shouted. 'A year from now, you'll see, we'll go together . . .' and now she dropped her voice so that I couldn't catch a single word.

So I got up finally from my shady spot and walked over to the other side of the path. But I turned once more and noticed to my surprise that lying in the dust by the fence was an enamelled plate just like those which surrounded the door of the village shop. A red lobster with huge claws seemed about to clutch its prey:

> Good advice for you:
> Use Otta shampoo!

As soon as dinner was over Mr Štěrbák appeared in the doorway, not in his little apron now, but in black trousers and a white shirt with a formal bow-tie, and announced that he had prepared a little surprise for all of us and would we please follow him.

Everybody sitting in the dining-room rose to their feet; even Father, who normally hurried straight from dinner to his calculations, walked down the few steps into the garden.

The red tables and chairs were arranged in a semi-circle and, as soon as we had sat down, Mr Štěrbák looked up to the dark sky and exclaimed: 'Let there be light!' At that moment coloured lightbulbs and Chinese lanterns lit up among the branches of the chestnut tree above our heads. We all caught our breath in surprise but before we could even utter a sound the light came on in a small window right up in the roof and there appeared unexpectedly the man who evidently loved not only fire but heights as well. He held an accordion, and from on high the fireman played to us the Joy Chorus from the 'Bartered Bride'. Not until he had finished did Mr Štěrbák bow to us and solemnly announce that with this music he was inaugurating his garden casino, also open at night, that he welcomed us all to it and hoped that he would have the pleasure of drinking with us to our enjoyment there. Already his wife was approaching with a circular tray with dewy glasses of beer on it. Dr Slavík no sooner got hold of his half-litre than he

57

stood up and made a speech in praise of Mr Štěrbák and the beer he dispensed; he also praised the dreaminess of summer evenings and the South Bohemian plain and asked us all never to forget this moment when fate let us sit together and be cheerful under the coloured lights.

Mr Feuerstein had meanwhile come down with his accordion, and the doctor, evidently exhausted by the seriousness of his speech, borrowed it and played for him and for us the song:

Whenever flames are started, by man or by God's ire,
The gallant firemen are on the scene again.
Only we weaklings ask the skies to quench the fire,
Put out the flames by swift torrential rain.

When he had finished, his wife leaned over to the elderly major-domo and in her gentle, deep voice requested him to tell us something of the old feudal days, and as the old man shyly resisted she added that his accounts had always cheered her up no matter how depressed she'd been. Mr Anton smiled at her and observed that this was probably because in the days he could remember life had been quite different, not necessarily better, he wouldn't say that, but certainly more tranquil. Then he related how some forty years earlier the Bezdřev pond was being fished and one young infantryman named Škédl got a little tipsy and with that Dutch courage he swiped an enormous pike and hid it under his jacket. But his jacket was rather short and he didn't notice that the pike's tail was showing. From the dam all the gentlemen were watching the fishing: the water bailiff, the fishery director, the estate manager and His Serene Highness himself.

I noticed my father scowling: Father didn't like gentlemen, he couldn't stand capitalists, big businessmen, bankers or farmers, and least of all did he have a taste for princes or their retainers.

And all those who watched the scene, Mr Anton continued his story as red and blue blossoms seemed to float over his white head, were breathlessly wondering what would happen when His Serene Highness caught sight of that pike's tail – which was exactly what happened very soon. The prince asked who that young man was and had him called over at once. As the poor chap, quite unsuspecting, presented himself, His Highness said: 'Škédl, next time a longer jacket or a shorter pike!'

The infantryman blushed but did not lose his presence of mind and replied: 'Yes, Your Serene Highness, next time a longer jacket!'

Mr Anton smiled at his own anecdote, but a little wistfully, and wondered whether, now that an end had been put to all those people, he would at least meet them again in the eternal kingdom of love. The doctor's wife clapped her hands and said that this was precisely the sort of story she'd wanted to hear, but I could see that my father was rather angry and about to object or say something, except that just then Dr Slavík called out: 'Well, major-domo, what would you like – a minuet or a polonaise?' He planted himself legs apart and the accordion in his hands sounded more like an organ or a harpsichord.

Mr Anton actually bowed in front of the doctor's wife and asked if she would honour him with this dance. She nodded graciously and permitted him to touch her shoulder, she gave him her hand and with slow but graceful steps the two began to turn in the semi-circle between our tables. They were immediately joined by the newly-wed Havels; and Mr Sodomka, the railwayman, stood up, walked up to our table and bowed to my mother. Mother, however, shook her head and informed him in a sad voice that unfortunately her heart was in such poor shape that she had to deny herself these pleasures. Mr Sodomka therefore just thanked her and went into the kitchen to get Mrs Štěrbáková.

So there were three couples dancing that old-time dance and I could see coloured butterflies flitting over the faces of the dancers, flying up and settling again on their hair, and I could see a golden flame every now and then flashing from the magnificent fingers of the doctor's wife. As I watched the dreamlike movements of her partner I realized that she was moving over the parquet floor of some palace ballroom, swirling under the candlelight among princes and princesses, among countesses and barons, carried away by the notes of the palace orchestra, and the doctor's wife too was vanishing into the distance, though I did not know what ground her light feet were touching, in what ballroom she was moving, even if I possibly suspected who her partner was. Meanwhile I remained there, right there under the branches of the chestnut-tree, with an orange Chinese lantern glowing above my head, a Chinese lantern round whose sides some junks were floating down a reedy river, and I wished that this moment would last forever so that I could, would, might be one of the dancers, bow to the doctor's wife and touch her fiery fingertips. It seemed to me that I was experiencing some strange intermingling of different periods, just as though I were gazing into a large iridescent bubble, into a glass ball in which everything intermingled: the ancient torch-light and the world with its fires of war and the quiet light of the Chinese lanterns and the coloured electric bulbs; and it even seemed to me that I might step into that sphere and, together with her, float up, and glide along some invisible edge that divided the indivisible and united the ununitable, become an aeronaut in a space reached only by the longing of souls.

The dancers had meanwhile led their ladies back to their seats, Dr Slavík had returned the accordion and was now calling over to Mr Sodomka to inquire what he was working on.

Mr Sodomka replied with seriousness that he was painting the drought.

How did one represent the drought? And the railwayman explained that he was doing so in the shape of a thin old woman who was eating up the ears of corn.

Then everybody started talking about the drought and the bad harvest; Mr Štěrbák observed that many of the farmers in the neighbourhood were gathering in less than they had planted. Mr Feuerstein added that all day long they had carted water by the tanker-load and sprinkled the beet on the estate, but the sun's heat was such that the water evaporated before it could reach the roots. If things continued like this, he forecast, the drought would cause a worse famine than the war had done.

I tried to listen to them but I was still inside my sphere of glass. I could not understand why anyone should be so terrified of hunger when people had survived so many disasters, when I myself had come to realize how very little was necessary to live on. I could not enter the area of their anxieties because spread out before me lay an area of totally boundless freedom.

Father by then was unable to refrain from joining in the conversation, declaring that there was no need for alarm because the fields would surely yield something, and whatever they yielded, unlike in the past, would now be fairly shared out.

'How do you mean?' Dr Slavík became alert.

Father explained that we were on the threshold of a new age when not only princes were disappearing but so were rich industrialists, landowners and big businessmen; there would be only the working people and they would share out fairly the goods produced by them.

'You really believe that all men will be equal?' the doctor asked my father.

'Everybody according to his deserts!' Father replied with conviction. 'But nobody will have the right to appropriate the fruits of anybody else's labour, nobody will be permitted to exploit anybody else. And those who already have accumulated property like that will be compelled to part with it again!'

'All that's Utopia!' Dr Slavík was almost shouting now. 'You may rob one lot to give to another, but nothing will change in the world. Except that another lot will be poor and a different lot rich!'

So they began to argue, and the doctor proved to Father

that he didn't know the ape called man at all, and that this ape in contrast to all other apes, and indeed all other animals, would never be content or satisfied. Anyone with the ability, the opportunity and the means to do so would start accumulating property again at the expense of the rest. That was the rock on which all reforms and revolutions foundered – but only after a lot of blood had been shed. Father on the other hand maintained that man was basically good and had only been spoiled by his environment, by property or by poverty, by poor education, religious obscurantism and a lot of other prejudices and atavistic remnants. But all this would be changed as soon as people were freed from their dependence on property, as soon as they had no more than what they needed for their lives.

At this point Mr Štěrbák joined in: he wanted to know if he would then be allowed to own his inn; Father explained that he'd probably not be allowed to own his inn but he'd surely be allowed to be the manager. Mr Štěrbák tossed his head and declared that he wouldn't give a monkey's fart to be the manager of his own inn, he'd rather look after the horses, and Dr Slavík remarked that this was exactly what would happen: innkeepers would be stablelads and stablelads innkeepers, or, worse still, doctors would shoe the horses and blacksmiths would treat the people.

It was obvious that this remark annoyed my father, but he controlled himself. He merely expressed regret that the doctor's otherwise clear mind had been so misled. The opposite was true: for the first time in history everybody would do what he really wanted to do; to this day a lot of people were compelled by their origin or position to do work they'd never wished to do. A lot of clever people were unable to finish their education because they were too poor; he for instance had only got his engineering diploma by an all-out effort, giving private lessons at night in order to keep himself. But now for even the poorest of the poor all obstacles would be removed, a lot of capable individuals would get an education and invent further technical improvements, so that an ever growing number of ever cheaper articles would be produced, and these would in turn liberate people from toil and help them in their struggle against nature. And now Father was really in his element. He described the marvellous machines that would fundamentally change the character of life. Giant generators producing enough electricity, not only to light cities but to drive hundreds of thousands and later millions of motors and automatic tools which, virtually without human assistance and usually without heavy labour, would produce an abundance of shoes, textiles, kitchen utensils as well as refrigerators, washing machines, motor cars and combine harvesters. And he described how supersonic aircraft would carry us in a matter of hours from one continent to another, he spoke of machines which would build roads and houses, mine ore and coal, of new synthetic materials to replace silk, timber and metal, which because they'd be manufactured from coal and oil would be plentiful, and shortages would rapidly disappear from the world, and as soon as shortages disappeared, Father was now warming to his subject, there would no longer, in a new society governed by the people, be any reason for hankering after property, no envy, hatred or hostility, there'd be no cause for wars because ultimately the fundamental cause of every war had been greed and the attempt to rob the vanquished. There would therefore be peace and trust, an age of comradeship would dawn, and eventually nations would vanish as would the frontiers between them, and man's homeland quite simply would be the world – yes, he would go so far as to say: at last a world in which human beings would live in dignity and happiness.

Father was talking with such fire that everybody was listening to him attentively, and I felt proud that he was able so beautifully and convincingly to portray our life in the future; I liked that life because it seemed to me to be exalted and pure, unsullied by any meanness or worldliness.

When Father had finished, Dr Slavík said only: 'Then

rings the bell, my friend; the fairy-tale is at an end.' Then he turned to Father and added: 'You're not a bad person, Engineer, I'm sure you believe all you're saying – but I hope for your sake you won't live to see it.'

'Live to see what?'

'The paradise you've described for us,' said the doctor. 'I hope you won't have to live in it.'

'We'll all live to see it, we'll all live in it,' Father said prophetically.

The great master Balzac wrote:

And the happiness enjoyed by Lucien was the fulfilment of the dreams of poets starving in some garret without a single sou. Esther, the ideal of the courtesan in love, reminded Lucien somewhat of Coralie, the actress with whom he had lived for a year, but she totally overshadowed her. All loving and devoted women long to live like a pearl on the seabed, seeking out hidden corners and disguises; but with most of them this is a charming caprice, one that is prettily talked about, a proof of love which they would so much wish to give but do not in fact give. Whereas Esther, who was still reliving the morning after the first amorous bliss and who was still under the effect of Lucien's first passionate glance, had not, throughout four years, exhibited the least bit of curiosity . . . Not even during the most intoxicating delights did she abuse the infinite power which a woman who is loved derives from the rekindled desire of her lover . . .

The next morning I overslept. When I came down to breakfast there was only the gloomy Mr Halama left in the dining-room. I said good morning to him and he turned his ashen, sun-resistant face to me: 'You didn't feel like waking up either?'

I didn't know what to reply, so I said I'd been reading late.

'But what else can a man do?' he continued, just as though he had not heard my answer. '*Der Mann muss hinaus ins feindliche Leben!*' (Man has to go out into a hostile world!) His German sounded perfect to me. He disregarded me to such an extent that he didn't even bother to conceal his origin from me. I turned rigid and didn't know what to do in order not to betray my excitement. Fortunately the inn-keeper's wife appeared just then with a mug of milk and informed me that my parents had gone down to the river and expected me to follow them.

Mr Halama got up. As he moved past me he gave me an imperceptible wave of his hand and left the room.

I quickly gulped my milk, grabbed my roll and hurried out of the inn.

I just managed to catch sight of him as he moved off rapidly down the track that led to the station. Without a moment's hesitation I set out in the same direction.

The sun was now lying heavily on the fertile plain as I waded through the dust on the little path across the fields. The sweat was trickling down into my eyes but I firmly kept in sight the figure in front of me. Only when he stepped into the once red but now rather grimy building was I able to stop. In any case I couldn't follow him into the station if I didn't want to be spotted by him and give away the fact that I was shamelessly following him.

So I sat down on the hot wild thyme by the path and gazed up at the clear sky. Just then my attention was caught by a strange gleaming sphere in the distance, moving at a height at which, when it rained, the clouds would sail, and rapidly approaching me. I soon made out a hot-air balloon with a yellow gondola swinging beneath it. It floated majestically, silently, almost gently, and it was now near enough for me to read the gold-coloured lettering on its skin:

MORE

At that moment a whitish rope-ladder was flung over the rail, but of course it did not come anywhere near enough to reach the ground, even though the balloon was now noticeably losing height as it drifted directly over the smoky railway station building. I watched the ladder waving in the wind, then a figure swung itself up on the rail. Of course I couldn't make out the face but judging by the slender waist and short, silver skirt it was clearly a girl. For a moment she stood at that terrifying altitude, then she grabbed the rope-ladder and swiftly climbed down to its bottom rung, and to my horror let herself even further down with her bare feet dangling in the void while her hands gripped the rung. Suspended like that she began to swing over the deep emptiness, then she slipped her head between the two lowest rungs and flicked into a neat handstand, her body arched like a bow. I realized she was an acrobat performing her star turn. The balloon dropped a little lower and I saw someone throwing a yellowish package overboard; this hurtled straight down towards the railway line but before hitting the ground it suddenly seemed to divide: its upper half turned into a brightly coloured parachute which billowed out over a dark box and gently sailed down to earth.

I should have run across to the spot where it came down but I just couldn't tear my eyes off that girl in the heavens. She was still doing her handstand, but her legs were now extended horizontally so she formed a large letter T. Next she hooked her knees over a rung, let go with her hands and slowly moved her body away from the ladder; with her arms extended in front of her she lay on the air as if she were swimming. She'd now swum right over my head and if some accident happened, if the rung she was holding on to snapped, or if she slipped out of it, she'd drop straight into my arms. I stood there in ecstasy watching the balloon moving away, shifting towards the fiery disc of the sun and probably vanishing from my sight forever.

Only for a moment did I drop my eyes to the ground to glance towards the station – I had completely forgotten about it, I was oblivious of what had been happening there, whether a train had arrived or departed while I was gazing at the sky, whether anyone had shown up or disappeared. When I looked up again, the sky was once more empty, indeed there wasn't a single cloud in it, and all at once I felt like crying with the loneliness that had suddenly over-whelmed me on that wide, parched, dusty field.

When I got to the station, I found it deserted. There was no trace of Mr Halama or even of the parcel that had sailed down.

I set out on my homeward journey by a round-about route. I went towards the Old River, where the track was lined by ancient shrunken willows and massive elms. Here and there a fisherman was silently sitting in their shade, closely watching his motionless float. Among the anglers I spotted Dr Slavík.

As soon as he saw me he exclaimed:

> 'By the stream Annette was sitting
> While on the other bank Eileen was sh–, sh–
> outing joyfully at her . . . '

Then he asked me if I'd ever been under a girl's skirts. I shook my head while he hauled in his line, produced a piece of cheese from a tin of Hagenbeck tea and replaced his bait. 'No need to pretend to each other,' he remarked and made a fresh cast. 'I too was seventeen once. Know Pilsen at all?'

I did not know Pilsen at all, and he began to reminisce about his studies there. He'd lived by the theatre and his window had looked straight out on the dressing rooms. Whenever they'd staged *Aida* or *Carmen* the place would be full of girls from the chorus, and some of them knew he was watching from his window and changed so he could see everything.

The doctor leaned back against the tree-trunk, had a quick look at the lifeless float and lit a cigarette. 'Let me tell you something, student. A man's a fool at that age and does a lot of stupid things – things he prefers not to remember. But the most stupid thing of all is to believe that women are people like you. No,' he shook his head vigorously and looked in a southerly direction, to where a little while before the balloon with the beautiful acrobat had disappeared. 'I'm not saying they're worse or they're better, but they are different. You get fooled by the fact that they have a similar head, hands and feet, and even from their lips there may come words such as you might use, so you begin to believe you can communicate with them, that their heads might conceivably produce a thought like your own. And by the time you discover that this isn't so, because their heads serve a totally different purpose, it's too late.'

Just then the float jerked, the doctor bit back another bitter thought, flicked his cigarette into the water, gripped his rod and snatched it up. Then he reeled his line in until a twisting little fish appeared at its end. The doctor removed the hook from its mouth, weighed it in his hand, observed that he was a whopper who'd evidently got fat on wartime rations and threw it back into the river. I'd expected him to continue his lecture on the total dissimilitude of women but he suddenly glanced up at the sky, discovered with a shock that it was nearly midday and he had to be in Chlum for the dress rehearsal first thing after lunch. The grand performance of the *Strakonice Bagpiper* was taking place the following day, and he had the honour to play in the orchestra. Was I coming to see it?

I didn't know what my parents would decide but the doctor thought that, if the rest of my family were not interested in the performance, then surely I could go without them. He had to be in Chlum first thing in the morning but I could escort his wife there.

I agreed so enthusiastically that I was afraid I was betraying my emotions, and hurriedly remarked that Mr Halama had taken the train somewhere today. I was surprised he was not staying for the performance.

The doctor flung his fishing bag over his shoulder, picked up his rod and said: 'Don't you worry, he'll be back tonight!'

I was impatiently waiting for him to add something in explanation but he began to sing to himself in a low voice:

'The fishpond's ready to be drained;
When I go out my Mum looks strained . . .'

We walked along the river, which meandered through the meadows. Here and there we had to force our way through undergrowth and reeds, and I didn't have the courage to start a conversation, when all of a sudden the doctor turned to me and said how right I'd been to mention that glum pharmacist because Mr Halama was a perfect example of what a woman could do to a man. Mr Halama had been a cheerful chap, with an attractive bachelor pad in an attic in Žižkov, the walls covered with picture postcards and posters of pretty girls; interesting books, retorts and bottles with poisons all over the place, in short a chap who had some standing in his profession. Every so often he'd bring out some floor polish of his own, or some washable wall-paint, or some perfumed soap called *clamor amoris* which, as no doubt I knew, meant call of love. Pink and perfumed for women and green and perfumed for men. He'd written a leaflet proving that anyone washing themselves all over with that soap would become irresistible to the opposite sex, and no doubt he'd sold the product to that particular broad because, the moment he caught sight of her, he was lost, even though the woman was as ugly as sin, eight years older and two heads shorter than he was. He'd even installed her in his pleasant flat, let her into his shop, and that wasn't all, he also began to be at her beck and call and to pander to her every whim. On top of it all she was jealous of him. So jealous that one day he could stand it no longer, threw a scene like on the stage, picked up his shabby briefcase and fled from his home, from whose walls the pictures of the pretty girls had long disappeared to make room for ornamental little hangings embroidered in gold with such idiotic things as 'If confidence you don't profess – you're far from finding happiness', or 'Contentment and no strife – bridges to a happy life'. So he came here to get away from it all and recover a bit. But how could he recover when from the very first moment he was just waiting for that monster of a woman to claim him back?

The surprising thing was that she hadn't turned up yet –

usually she'd appear within three days, five at the most, whereas this time Mr Halama had been on strike here for a whole week. To start with he'd sulked in his room, on the fourth day he'd sneaked out by the back door to the station, and this time he'd probably gone to look for her in Třeboň. God knows what's happened, the doctor reflected; maybe that female dwarf had really picked up some chap and wasn't going to turn up at all, so that Mr Halama would remain permanently sentenced to a bachelor existence at Mr Štěrbák's inn.

While I was coping with my disappointment at this mundane explanation of the incident the doctor once more broke into song:

> 'The nets are drawn, the fish are caught;
> Why am I weeping, why so distraught?
> Fishermen, fishermen, take me to sea
> To stifle the yearning that ravages me.'

That evening my brother at last got his wish. Mother had bought a canful of milk from Mr Pavelec, I was carrying a blackened army billycan that Father had liberated somewhere in Mecklenburg during the final days of the war, and my brother asked to be allowed to carry the tin with the picture of a pretty Dutch girl in clogs.

At the forest's edge we built a fire, made a low support and hung our billycan from it. As soon as the flames began to leap up Mother started to unpack the sandwiches and proposed that we should sing. But, as in our family no one had an ear for music except Father, who didn't like singing or at any rate regarded song as something that kept you from useful work, her proposal remained unanswered.

The fire was crackling beautifully; now and again it ejected a fistful of sparks. Mother ceremoniously opened the Van Houten packet and with a teaspoon scooped out a minute quantity of the precious powder and sprinkled it into a glass. Father considered the moment suitable for a bit of a lecture on the world and what was happening in it: he explained that, now that we were at peace once more and the war had ended with a great victory of the greatest socialist country, one that occupied a whole sixth of the globe, everything was changing and we'd be building a new order in our country too.

When we talked about serious matters Father expected us to listen to him, to hang upon his every word, but I noticed that my brother couldn't tear his eyes away from the billycan into which Mother had just poured the brown cocoa mixture and my own gaze wandered off every so often around the landscape which was gradually veiling itself in mist and shadow.

Of course it wouldn't be easy, Father continued, the revolution had only just begun, the people would have to chase away the last remnants of the exploiters and settle accounts with the new rich, all those national administrators, peasants, fat merchants or even doctors – Father added one more profession for Mother's benefit.

At that moment I caught sight in the distance of a white horse with a black mane approaching at a gallop from the village, its rider's long hair flying in the wind. As they came closer the rider seemed familiar: at first I thought I recognized the girl acrobat, and the thought that I would see her face excited me. But, as the horse got nearer, the rider's figure, now leaning forward, with golden hair flying about a proudly erect head, seemed even more familiar and I was certain now that I recognized my neighbour from Mr Štěrbák's inn.

But that would all be accomplished, Father continued while the air, until then smelling of smoke, was increasingly filled with the intoxicating perfume of chocolate, and no one would be able to stop us from creating a totally different, better and more humane society.

The horse – as if making a semi-circle around us – was now aiming for the next patch of woodland beyond the over-ripe corn. I was afraid that in a moment I would lose sight of her, just as before lunch the gleaming balloon had vanished, but as she got to the first trees and was engulfed by their now almost opaque shade the rider pulled up, and I saw a dim figure stepping out from the forest, reaching up to her and lifting her down off the horse.

'And I believe,' Father was saying, 'that you will live to see such a society, and not only live to see it . . .'

'It's boiling over!' my brother interrupted in a mighty voice. 'Quick, do something!'

The figure entwined its arms with the blue arms of the rider and in a few long strides carried her off into the darkness of the forest.

Father grabbed the billycan, Mother passed him the mugs and Father carefully poured the beverage into them. Then everybody was loud in praise of the delicious stuff, while all the time I was looking towards the woods, wanting to be there, to intertwine my arms with those exquisite arms, to press my lips not against the hot metal but against other hot lips.

The great master Sholokhov wrote:

The light that hit Grigory's eyes blinded him for a second; he shaded them with his palm and turned when he heard the growing noise in the corner of the stables. With his hand touching the wall he walked over; a patch of sunlight was dancing on the floor and over the mangers. Grigory strode along, blinking his sun-blinded eyes. That joker Zharkov was walking towards him. As he walked he was buttoning up the front of his sagging trousers and nodding his head.

'What are you doing here? . . . What's going on?'

'Better hurry!' whispered Zharkov, breathing the stench of an unwashed mouth into Grigory's face. 'Over there . . . it's great! . . . The boys have dragged Franya in . . . pinned her down . . .' Zharkov guffawed but he stopped at once as his back hit the beams of the stable, where Grigory had flung him. Grigory was now running towards the noise and the whites of his widened eyes, which were getting accustomed to the gloom, showed fear. In the corner, where the horse blankets were folded,

was a big crowd of cossacks – the whole of No. 1 platoon . . .
Lying on the ground, unconscious, her legs horribly forced open
and shimmering white in the dark, lay Franya. She was not
moving at all. Her head was entangled in the blankets and her
ripped skirt was pulled up to her breasts. A cossack was just
getting up off her, holding on to his trousers; without looking at
his comrades and with a crooked grin he walked over to the wall,
making room for another.

In the end I really was the only member of our family to go
to the performance of the *Strakonice Bagpiper*. Mother had a
headache and Father wasn't interested in theatricals. My
brother, admittedly, made the daring remark that he'd
never yet seen an amateur performance but Mother soon
silenced him: surely he wasn't having a holiday in order to
breathe foul air in some spittle-filled hall? My brother was
only ten, so he had no choice but to submit. So, wearing my
only suit which, thanks to my rake-like figure, hung on me
as if I were a scarecrow, I was able to stride along beside the
doctor's perfumed and beautiful wife. The way to Chlum
was along an old avenue of trees, and because the sun was
about to set the shadows of the trees merged and totally
covered us with their cool blanket.

Millie and Rosie, the twins whom I'd still not learnt to tell
apart, were walking or rather tripping some distance ahead
of us, but it seemed to me that the doctor's wife liked it that
way because she could have a nice chat with me. She asked
me about the books I always carried around with me, she
even dragged out of me that I'd written some poems and
short stories. She immediately demanded that I should
recite one of my poems to her but I declined – not so much
from modesty as from fear that I might not remember it
properly and would start stammering embarrassingly. But
she, even though she had no opportunity to judge the
extent of my skill or lack of it as an artist, expressed delight
at walking by the side of a young poet. Maybe she'd
forgotten her recent bitter condemnation of all writing

73

because she said that the student she'd mentioned also used to write poetry and had actually written a poem for her album.

> When 'midst life's woes and tribulations
> No joy nor pleasure you discern,
> Then raise your eyes to sunlit summits,
> Have faith: your fortune soon will turn!

I would probably regard these lines as commonplace but they had moved her at the time and she had often recalled them when she'd felt low. And she added that although she had never written any poetry herself, she didn't want me to get the wrong impression – after all, she'd had piano and singing lessons, as well as horse-riding, and French lessons from a private tutor. Her father had even thought of sending her to the conservatoire but then the war had interfered with that. He'd been an ordinary butcher, a little fierce but a good man and fond of animals. He was forever bringing home some stray cat or dog, and they'd had to look after it until someone came to collect it, but he wanted his children to get on in life. And indeed one of her brothers was a lawyer and the other a chemical engineer, and her younger sister had graduated from the business college; only she herself had dropped out because the war had come and because as a girl of seventeen she'd lost her head and been carried away by a young doctor running after her. If only she'd known what she was in for!

Now she wasn't quite twenty-five and the best part of her life was behind her. If those two girls proved as stupid as she'd been, she'd soon be a grandmother.

She produced a handkerchief from her handbag and dabbed her eyes, then she looked at me and asked if I didn't think this was a beautiful avenue of trees and if we continued along it we'd come to a spot from where the golden turrets of a fairy-tale castle could be seen, at least in the distance. I didn't think that at all likely but I nodded agreement. At that point a deep sigh escaped from her chest, she stopped and leaned against the trunk of a tree. The twins had disappeared somewhere ahead, but she seemed to have forgotten about them or at least wasn't looking in their direction. She was looking at me with her large, dark pupils.

Her gaze confused me, I didn't know what to do, whether to say something gentle or perhaps step up to her and . . . The thought that I might try to embrace her and perhaps even kiss her disturbed me so much and caught me so unawares that I dropped my eyes and didn't even dare look at her. So we stood motionless and in silence until eventually the doctor's wife moved and whispered: 'You're still so young. And so inexperienced!' She extended her palm towards me, still clutching her handkerchief, but halfway through the movement she changed her mind, withdrew her hand again, opened her handbag and, as she replaced her handkerchief, something rustled like bits of paper. When her hand re-emerged it enclosed a glittering object. She handed it to me. It was a large boiled sweet wrapped in gold tinfoil.

The performance took place in the local Sokol club-house. It was clearly about to start since the hall, I noticed, was full of people.

The doctor's wife handed her coat in at the cloakroom. It was only then that I realized why she had taken it along at all: her dress was sleeveless and its neckline plunged low, front and back, not so much covering her as making her look naked.

We hurriedly made our way to the third row where our seats were. I froze in anticipation of how we'd sit but the doctor's wife placed the twins on her left and me on her right, produced a mirror and compact from her handbag, licked her lips, patted her fair hair and moved the gold four-leafed clover on her necklace so that it almost slipped into the cleavage between her breasts, then she turned to the twins, offered them sweets in silver paper, and only then turned to me to ask if I was satisfied with my seat. But

75

in doing so she smiled at me in such a way that I immediately, if only for a moment, soared upwards and out of the hall; I was flying with her like a bird, like a balloon, across the wide sky, and our arms entwined and our lips touched.

The lights were being dimmed, the blue velvet of the curtain was vibrating with impatience, the entire hall was humming with anticipation; the orchestra, placed below the left part of the stage, was moaning excitedly. When it was completely dark I saw the flashing baton in the hand of an unknown conductor and at the same moment I spotted the massive figure of Dr Slavík among the musicians. I wanted to point him out to his wife but just then the music started, the doctor's wife leaned back in her chair, her eyes half-closed, and I looked at the curtain which was slowly and jerkily parting.

As the first few figures of gaping children and little girls emerged, the noise in the hall grew and delighted shouts were heard. When the curtain was fully drawn back to reveal the whole backcloth I, like everybody else, was speechless: for there, right before our eyes, in all its glory stood Mr Štěrbák's inn, complete with its sign and the letters forming the rhymed slogan trickling out of the carp's mouth. The doctor's wife leaned towards me, breathed on me with her fragrant mouth and whispered that the set had been painted by Mr Sodomka. Just then I caught sight of the red-haired fireman, Mr Feuerstein, entering in a pale-blue military uniform to the applause of an audience who were enthusiastic even before the start of the performance.

The doctor's wife turned her fragrant mouth away again and looked at the stage; I too looked in that direction, trying to take in what was being said and enacted there, but I was unable to concentrate on the problems of someone else's love. What was I to do? Surely I daren't hope that such an immature, unknown and poor schoolboy like me could interest such an experienced and beautiful woman? And even if I did hope, didn't such a relationship with a married woman run counter to all my moral principles?

At that moment the orchestra had a noisy entry and Mr Feuerstein took up a position at the very edge of the stage and began to sing that money made the world go round. As soon as he'd finished his couplet the audience applauded so enthusiastically that Mr Feuerstein took off his army cap, bowed, waved, and even blew a kiss to someone in the auditorium.

The doctor's wife was clapping too, and when Mr Feuerstein eventually ran off the stage she shifted a little in her chair and I could feel her calf lightly touching mine. I froze into immobility, I almost stopped breathing, as if made of stone I remained in that gap between the seats. If she didn't move her leg away at once then she hadn't touched me by accident, even though she seemed to be watching, and indeed closely and attentively, what was happening on the stage. I managed, without moving at all, to press my calf more firmly against hers so that I seemed to feel the warmth of her skin through the wood-fibre material of my trousers. O God!

Just then I noticed that her right hand, which had until then rested on her knee, was moving and slipping into the little gap between our chairs and I realized what I had to do: slowly, very slowly I moved my hand towards hers until I felt that as yet inexperienced contact: I felt her fingers brushing over mine, interlinking with mine, and our fingers rapidly turned into a joint bird's wing on which we were able to soar up, to rise, to hover above the nocturnal tops of chestnuts and limes, under the summer stars, sink down on the moss and cover ourselves with it to conceal our total nudity, our sin, our passion.

I was still looking at the stage where some figures in bright folk costume were moving about, where at one moment a piece of scenery collapsed and smacking kisses were exchanged to the delight of the audience – but I was lost by then. Lost to everything that was happening, that would be happening, to everything that was not touched by that warm hand.

During the interval I was quite unable to talk, or even to get up in case my arousal would be obvious. The doctor's wife went off somewhere with the twin girls, and I waited meekly for her to return, for the lights to go out again, for the world around us to be veiled by a flood of words, and for her to slip her hand into mine once more.

What would I do next?

After the performance, Dr Slavík was waiting for us. He called out to us not to go off anywhere because he'd secured seats on a cart to take us home. He led us behind the club-house and there stood an almost new wagon with rubber tyres, with two geldings slumbering in the shafts.

We clambered aboard, a few strangers got on after us, and the last one to turn up, welcomed with noisy shouting, was the red-haired Mr Feuerstein. He took hold of the reins, said something to the horses, and the vehicle moved off smoothly.

Dr Slavík produced his trumpet from its case, placed it against his lips and sounded the retreat; perhaps it was this penetrating sound that sent the geldings into a gallop.

When the doctor had finished his bugle call, he asked us if we'd noticed that a whole scene had been dropped in the third act because Vocílka was nowhere to be found. The red-haired Mr Feuerstein, who had taken the parts not only of Šavlička but of Vocílka as well, turned back to us from the horses and explained that at the end of the second act his throat had dried up so much that he was certain he wouldn't be able to utter another word and could not make his next entrance. And, although he'd quenched that terrible thirst in the interval, he hadn't been able to cope with the consequences of that quenching, and so the inevitable happened.

Everybody laughed while I, in that nocturnal darkness, was looking at the doctor's wife, now sitting by her husband's side, pressing herself against him. That ambiguity, the need to pretend, filled me with despair. I felt like jumping off the wagon and escaping to some distant place,

78

into the fields which were already covered by the evening mist, to be alone, not to see or hear anything, not to have to get off with them or say goodnight to them in cold and unemotional words.

The great master Maupassant wrote:

She did not say anything either, she was sitting motionless in her corner. If it were not for the fact that each time some light penetrated into the carriage he could see the glitter of her eyes he would have thought she was sleeping.

'What is she thinking of?' He knew very well that he must not speak, that one single word would disrupt the silence and carry away his hopes; yet he lacked the courage, the courage for sudden and violent action.

Suddenly he felt that she had moved her leg. That abrupt sharp movement possibly signified impatience, perhaps a challenge. An almost imperceptible twitch sent a shiver through his whole body, suddenly he turned, threw himself on her, with his mouth sought her lips and with his hands tried to touch her body.

She uttered a cry, but softly, she tried to collect herself, resist, push him away, but then she yielded as though she had lost all strength for further resistance. But the carriage soon stopped at the house where she lived. Duroy was taken by surprise, he was unable to think of passionate words, to thank her, bless her and express his grateful love. But Madame de Marelle did not get up, she did not move at all, she was so confused by what had just happened . . .

Eventually she got out, stumbling, but without uttering a word. He rang the bell, and when the door opened he asked excitedly: 'When can I see you again?'

She whispered so softly he could scarcely make out her words: 'Come to lunch tomorrow!' . . .

He gave the cabman a five-franc piece and set out quickly and triumphantly, his heart overflowing with joy.

At last he had a married woman!

The next morning everybody in the dining-room was talking about the performance. Even my mother asked questions – but when I answered as though in a dream she noticed my pallor and the rings under my eyes and was immediately alarmed that in that overcrowded hall I might have caught some sickness, and hadn't she said I shouldn't go anywhere.

If only she knew what sickness had got into me.

I had lain awake most of the night and it had seemed unlikely to me that I would ever know the relief of tranquil sleep again.

I glanced furtively at the next table. The doctor's wife was just spreading some butter on a roll. Her suntanned face was glowing with health. Her husband, her unsuspecting deceived husband, was drinking his coffee, smiling, no doubt mentally enjoying one of his improper anecdotes.

During the night I had realized that my position was untenable, just as my action was scarcely excusable. Her action, of course, was a lot more excusable. Life at the side of the doctor might indeed seem interesting or even amusing, but what torture it must be for such a delicate and sensitive woman! After all, as I understood him, the doctor didn't even regard women as human beings. And to listen to his lubricious talk! Small wonder she was seeking the golden turrets of fair-tale castles, that she was longing for someone to give her kindness, love and support. But what could I give her? That's what I'd have to say to her. That I'd long to love her, to be with her, by her side, but that I couldn't. That I had no right to step into her life, where I would only destroy what little she had left.

Again I cast a furtive look towards her table. She was eating a roll and explaining something to one of her indistinguishable daughters. She probably hadn't looked at me all morning, just as if I weren't here at all, just as if last night never happened. Or was she already overcome with horror at what we'd started together?

I promised my parents I would come down to the river later in the morning, and returned to my room. After my sleepless night, exhaustion came over me. I stretched out on my bed and for a while speculated what I would do if Dr Slavík spoke to me or even asked me to escort his wife somewhere. From outside came the distant gurgle of water and the squealing of children; they were like a lullaby.

I was awakened by a soft knock at the door. I leapt from my bed and, before I could do anything at all, the door opened very quietly.

She was standing in the doorway: 'You were asleep?'

I said I'd been lying down and meditating.

'What were you meditating about?' Her blue blouse was half unbuttoned so I could see the tanned skin of her breasts.

'Nothing in particular.'

'Did you at least think a little about me?'

How splendidly she stood there, how nobly she held her head.

It had occurred to her, she said, that I might lend her something nice to read. Her husband, as usual, had disappeared with his rod, the girls were by the river, and she got bored just lying there and staring at the sky.

She was still standing in the door, holding a pair of dark sunglasses, and the fragrance of lilies-of-the-valley gently floated over to me.

At last I pulled myself together and asked her in. I certainly had enough books.

Which of them should I recommend to her?

I had started nearly all of them, all were good, even excellent, it depended on what she was looking for in a book. (What I was looking for I wouldn't have admitted even under torture.)

She said she liked reading about love, about some great, sad love. She was standing so close to me that she lightly touched me with her hip.

I must offer her some of these books, but for God's sake how could I speak about books now?

'You won't advise me?' She looked at me and acted as if that saddened her. Her face was quite close to mine. I had never seen any woman's face so close.

81

She raised her sunglasses to her eyes as if to put them on, but then she changed her mind.

How does one go about kissing a strange woman? Should I just move closer to her and without a by-your-leave touch her lips with mine? Suppose she was offended? Suppose she cried out?

But suppose she was not offended and did not cry out? What then?

'No one's ever wanted to advise me!' She reached out sideways towards the table to put down her glasses, but she must have misjudged the distance because the glasses clattered to the floor.

She bent down at the same time as I and in that movement almost totally revealed her breasts: for a moment I caught sight of them, whitish on a suntanned chest, magnificent, desirable, round, dreamed-of and so often imagined, and I realized that I could touch them. She'd come to me, that's why she'd come to me, not for any books. And so, instead of her glasses, I reached for her shoulder. She now sank down on to her knees, embraced me with her arms so that for an instant she pressed me firmly to her breasts, and hurriedly kissed me.

Then she opened her arms again, reached out for her glasses, retreated from me and stood up. 'Not now, not now, it's too light here,' she whispered; 'and somebody might come!'

She went over to the table as if nothing had happened, picked up one of the books and said she'd borrow that one. I tried to detain her and kiss her once more, but she slipped away and said that I had no sense at all. The house was full of people and I mustn't do that. Then she left the room.

The rest of the day I didn't think of anything else. She'd said: Not now, not now, it's too light here, and somebody might come. It followed therefore that once it was dark, once everybody was asleep, it would be yes. She'd be waiting for me, she'd be lying on that bed on the far side of my wall, and I'd come to her as so many men before me had

82

come to the woman they loved, I'd come and I'd act like them.

And how, in point of fact, would I act? And what would happen next?

It was in the middle of dinner, the dining-room was again full, when a black Praga with TAXI on it suddenly pulled up in front of the inn.

The car snatched me momentarily out of the labyrinth of my single-track thoughts. I watched its door open and a tiny, bony woman with a piled-up bun of greying hair jump out from it. With her right hand she was gathering up her long skirt as if about to wade across an invisible stretch of water. She said something quickly to the driver and then charged ahead in the direction of our inn.

As she stepped through the door everybody, as if in response to some inaudible command, fell silent and looked at her. Only from Mr Halama's throat came a muffled scream, or rather a groan, and he pushed his chair back and got up.

The dwarf woman scurried between the tables and stopped in front of him. At that moment, maybe she was standing on tiptoe, she seemed to have grown in height and at the same time to have swollen menacingly, then she drew back her right hand and through the dining-room rang the smack of a slapped face. 'You bastard, you shocking, shameless bastard,' she addressed Mr Halama; 'is that the way to behave? Leave me to look after the shop and you rush off to chase your floozies!'

'But, darling,' said Mr Halama in his perfectly enunciated Czech. He was rubbing his left cheek and attempting a smile.

'Your bag,' the woman screamed at him, by now shrunk back into her minute shape, 'and look sharp!' She stepped aside a little and Mr Halama, with a frozen but, so it seemed to me, happy smile, walked through between the tables, finding time to stop in the doorway and say, 'See you again!' to us all. Then, with the dwarf woman at his back, he left the dining-room.

Through the window Dr Slavík watched the witch make for the black saloon and accompanied her departure with the poem:

> 'A man with a shrew for a wife
> Found her nagging was wrecking his life.
> A rake used for grass
> He shoved right up her arse –
> And that was the end of all strife.'

I dared not look at the doctor's table to see his wife's reaction.

The doctor then called Mrs Štěrbáková and ordered drinks all round because we must all now drink to the poor husband of that witch, and also to all men who were beaten by their wives, and he raised his half-litre mug. I noticed gloomily that the doctor's wife, as soon as her glass was put in front of her, lifted it up with gusto, and, because I didn't drink, I told my parents that I was going to bed, and left the room.

It was only nine o'clock. I knew that I would have to wait patiently until everyone in the house was asleep. And when would that be? Around midnight or later still? And suppose someone didn't go to sleep at all? Suppose the doctor woke up in the night, stepped out into the corridor and saw me just entering his wife's room? What would he do?

He'd kill me probably! Grab me by my lapels and fling me out of the window. Or he'd challenge me to a duel. He looked the kind of chap who could fire a pistol, or at any rate a hunting rifle. Or he might inject me with some hitherto unknown poison: I'd lose consciousness at once and in the morning they'd find me stiff on my bed. And there'd be no investigation. After all, who'd think that I'd left this life in such a vile manner; who'd think that I'd decided to commit such a vile deed? She alone. Assuming she was still alive.

Anyway, why didn't they share a room?

I stretched out on my bed. I was fairly tired but I knew I wouldn't fall asleep. I listened to the sounds from the dining-room below, where voices were still raised in cheerful conversation. Then somebody climbed up the stairs – perhaps the Havels – and a door clicked on the landing.

So what would I do when she came up? Should I wait for her to undress and lie down? Should I knock? Someone might hear me knock; knocking on doors after midnight was a little unusual. But surely I couldn't walk in without knocking!

I could knock on the wall. Yes, I'd knock on the wall and maybe she'd reply. Then I'd get up and creep silently into her room. And what then? Talk? Or quite simply lie down by her side? We hadn't even told each other we were in love.

And her naked body would press against mine, I could feel the desired, unimaginable touch of a naked female body: the warmth, the softness and the smell! And whatever happened afterwards, let it happen! Let the ground open up or the door open – that single moment would be worth it all. O my dearest love. O irresistible temptation! I'll walk in, lie down with you, I'll embrace you like so many men before have embraced the woman they loved. I'll manage it, I'll certainly manage it too!

Perhaps I'd dropped off for a while after all because I hadn't heard either the creaking of the stairs or any footsteps on the landing until I heard the grating of her door. There was the click of a light switch and a voice – her voice – said something. Then I heard a second voice, and although I couldn't make out the individual words I immediately recognized it as belonging to the doctor. What business had he in her room when he never entered it otherwise?

I lay motionless on my bed, my face pressed to the wall, and for a while I could hear the voices. Then the bedsprings let out a groan as a body lay down on them, as two bodies lay down on them, and then I heard a persistent rhythmical creaking, I could hear the moaning of two voices, an unknown and yet so comprehensible a moaning which seemed to change to laughter. I buried my head in my pillow but I couldn't escape the sounds. How could she do

85

it, how could she allow it! Surely it was me she loved, not him, I knew that, I felt it. But she hadn't cried out now, she hadn't called for help – so how could she love me? She didn't love me either. I was only a plaything to her.

At last there was a moment's silence next door, then water from a jug, a voice, her alto amidst the splashing of water, I didn't want to hear it any more, I didn't want to see her any more, I'd never look at her again, I didn't really want to stay here any longer, I'd tell my parents I was going home tomorrow, but what would I do at home, I didn't want to go home either, I didn't want to go anywhere.

And what would she say if I were found here in a pool of blood in the morning, lifeless, dead for ever? I'd leave a letter on the table, no, not a letter, just a sheet of paper with a few words on it. I wouldn't even address her, I'd simply write:

I cannot live any longer in this perfidious, treacherous world . . .

But how to ensure that she was the first to enter my room? That she would catch sight of me lying here. Cry out and fling herself on my senseless body. Realizing what she had caused. Maybe I should address the note to her after all. Perhaps a better sentence would be: 'I am dying. No reproach. I forgive you.'

She'd probably cry. She'd swear never to do anything like that again, she'd kneel down by my body and start kissing me. Too late.

That was the main drawback of my contemplated deed: I wouldn't feel, hear or see anything. What good would her tears be to me then?

In the middle of the night I was once more awakened by the banging of a door, trampling feet on the stairs and loud shouting. Someone was calling for the doctor. I sat up in bed and looked around in surprise. What were they calling him for? Surely I was still alive and in one piece? Could it be that she . . . ? That she'd yielded to despair and had done what I'd only idly contemplated?

I quickly put on a shirt and trousers and slipped out on to the landing.

At the foot of the stairs stood Mrs Štěrbáková with some strange woman and Mr Havel. Dr Slavík's door was ajar and he called out that he was just coming. Then, also wearing only a shirt and trousers, his black bag in his hand, he ran down the stairs. Meanwhile Mrs Štěrbáková obligingly informed me that Mr Valeš had begun to throw up blood, a terrible lot of blood, he was probably in a bad way.

Strangely enough the vision of someone else's blood and someone else's death filled me with greater unease than the vision of my own tragic end. I returned to my room, shivering with cold. And she did not come out. Maybe she didn't even wake up. Or perhaps she was afraid she'd meet me.

For a while I thought of Mr Valeš, whom I didn't know but from whose mouth life was escaping, while I was lying there safe and sound, and I was seized by a cold vertigo as if I were standing on the crest of some sky-high mountain with precipices all round me.

I don't know when Dr Slavík returned but it was still dark. I heard his heavy footsteps on the landing. He was saying to someone: 'It's all over for him now, poor chap.'

Then complete and deep silence fell once more.

The funeral was on Saturday before lunch. Mrs Štěrbáková, in black, wrote out a notice to put on the door that lunch would be served an hour late, and she set out with her husband towards Mr Valeš's farm.

The bell was tolling.

In some embarrassment I put on my only suit. Of course I didn't have to go to the funeral of somebody I had never seen but I felt that it would be proper for me to go when everybody else from the house was going.

I'd even caught sight of *her* a moment earlier, wearing the same clothes as when she had sat next to me that evening, hurrying out after Mrs Štěrbáková. I hadn't said a word to her in all those days, apart from good morning. But I wasn't sure she'd even registered it. She seemed totally withdrawn, she was reading the book she'd taken away with her from my room, only twice had I spotted her by the river, and then once at breakfast it seemed to me that she was looking at me with a kind of astonishment or even wistfulness. But it's possible I misinterpreted that glance and she was simply dejected by the death of someone she had known and shared some secret with.

The bell was still tolling and villagers dressed in black were drifting past under my window. Then the deep notes of the funeral march floated across from the distance.

I only caught up with the cortège at the cemetery. The black hearse was drawn by four horses with black plumes. Behind the coffin walked the priest with a raised crucifix. Behind him came his acolytes and only then the rest of the people, large numbers of them, their deeply tanned faces – this summer the sun had scarcely gone behind a cloud – projecting from unaccustomed white collars. I recognized Mr Pavelec walking right at the head of the procession, then the schoolmaster and Mr Sodomka in his best railwayman's uniform, and Mr Feuerstein in the uniform of the voluntary fire brigade and Mr Anton actually in a dinner jacket; and there was Mr Štěrbák with his wife, and behind them I spotted *her* with her two daughters. I didn't know whom to join, so I fell in right at the very end and stopped with the rest of the cortège outside the open cemetery gate. The band was still playing and it was only then that among the musicians I recognized the massive figure of the doctor. Four men meanwhile had lifted the coffin from the hearse and, carrying it on their shoulders, passed through the cemetery gate, preceded only by the priest who was now praying aloud: '*Absolve, quaesumus Domine, animam famuli tui . . .*'

I stood by the wall, immediately inside the gate, and not far in front of me I saw a freshly-dug grave and then the hole in the ground disappeared behind a wall of bodies.

The bell was tolling directly ahead of me. People were still sorting themselves out among the graves when *she* suddenly separated from her daughters and walked over to me. I tried not to look at her, I stared at the spot where they were evidently lowering the coffin into the ground, but I couldn't not take notice of her: she stopped just a little way in front of me, bowed her fair head and clasped her hands together. I realized she was crying.

The priest was intoning, his voice came to me from a great distance but I was unable to concentrate on his words, I was thinking that at this moment she'd come here, she'd come to me, even though she could have chosen any other spot, and at the same time I felt the grippingly painful presence of death. Compared with that, what was my pain, my sadness?

And suddenly, as though the whole of life was passing through me, I saw what I had never seen before: a huge flower in the shape of a bell was opening out before us, fiery yellow like the sun but with a deep-blue centre, and I was stunned by the realization that this was possible: that she could yearn for me and make love to another and weep for another, yet that life was like that, that things panned out like that.

The priest finished and the whole crowd breathed Amen with him and then everybody sang a hymn. I dared to look at last and recognized a number of familiar faces: the milky head of Mr Anton and the severe features of the schoolmaster and the red hair peeping out from under Mr Feuerstein's fireman's peaked cap. The priest said another prayer and it struck me that I actually knew, or guessed, what these people were thinking about. The schoolmaster was reflecting that a man should find his proper place in life before it was too late; the doctor's wife was silently whispering to herself, we'll all meet there one day; Mr Feuerstein was sighing that what will be will be; and the old man with the milky hair was thinking of reunion in the eternal kingdom of love; while the doctor was already filling his broad chest with air to make his trumpet blare out, and I suspected, indeed I knew, what he was going to play. And at that moment a strange sense of relief came over me that these people, these strange souls, had come close to me. I was here with them and they were here with me under one heavenly roof.

The priest had fallen silent and the golden instruments sent endless reflections flashing into our saddened eyes and I stood there rigid, waiting for the first notes of the noble Hussite hymn.

And, when they did ring out, I shut my eyes but, even so the fire of the doctor's trumpet burned through my eyelids, its light washed over me and I could feel a great excitement taking hold of me. I opened my eyes, looked up, and there I saw it again: the silvery balloon approaching us, silently and smoothly floating towards us, descending out of the azure canopy, the rope-ladder dangling beneath it. When the balloon was directly overhead the acrobat, this time all in black, swung herself over the rail, slowly descended to the bottom rung of the ladder and stopped there motionless, as if paying her respects, as if she had turned into a statue of black marble.

I cast a furtive glance at my neighbour, to make sure she also saw the balloon, but she was staring at the ground and tears were rolling down her tanned cheeks. I moved sideways until I was standing next to her and with my finger-tips touched the back of her hand. Without looking up she squeezed my hand and I could feel my hand transforming itself into a wing. I was able to soar up, to fly, I could rock in the air like that balloon, I could fly away with it, choose any of the four points of the compass, but I remained where I was, I stopped above this small, painful, blessed piece of earth.

The Truth Game

I got on a Number 14 tram outside the Libeň Sokol club-house, clutching three carnations which were rapidly wilting in the afternoon's heat. The girl whom I'd been going out with for nearly a year, during which time she'd twice left me and had twice come back to me, had not turned up for our date. She'd probably decided to walk out on me for a third time.

For some time now I had been vainly trying to keep my certainties together.

After the end of the war, which had dragged on throughout my childhood like some poisonous snake, it seemed to me that a new age was beginning, one that would see the end of all injustice and suffering, and, unconsciously I longed to return to a state of innocence and of faith in the benign nature of a world in which good overcomes evil and truth always prevails.

If you long for something with all your heart then you'll find it – and I too found what I sought. Already I was living in that world, I had entered the promised land, I was carefree and happy in the simple knowledge that I no longer had to live in continual fear of a terminal sentence. I did not notice that a time of sentences had arrived once more.

But then, a few days after the death of the greatly celebrated Generalissimo, six Security men had come round to pick up my father. We hadn't seen him since. Charged with unbelievable economic crimes, he had been waiting for nearly four months in a jail at the other end of the country, waiting for his case to come up for trial.

His arrest crushed me. Although at an age that is regarded as the peak of rebellion against parental authority,

I still admired him. Ascetically modest, well-educated and indefatigable in his work, he believed in reason and in the new social order. So how could they now accuse him of criminal acts against that order?

A few days ago an old friend of mine from the Protestant Association brought me a folder with a much fingered typescript. After what had happened to our family, he suggested, we might find the text interesting.

The typescript, to my surprise, was not a religious tract but the translation of a biography of the recently deceased Generalissimo. It didn't give the translator; the author had a German name. I started reading it that same evening and after a few pages I was speechless. So far I'd only read the official biography. The giant, moreover, was closely linked in my memories with the end of the war and he'd gazed down on me solemnly from countless pictures: exalted and celebrated. Now I was reading about him as if he were some Napoleon who, on his road to personal power, had betrayed the Revolution and his fellow-fighters, a student priest who didn't complete his course, a man who'd diluted the ideals of his predecessors in a few miserable and trivial pamphlets, a cruel despot who'd never hesitated to send to his death anyone who'd stood in his path.

It occurred to me that I should really destroy such a blasphemous text immediately but I didn't want to destroy something that didn't belong to me. So I took the folder and after a moment's hesitation put it in the cupboard which housed the gas meter and covered it up with some rags. I was determined to return the libellous piece of writing to its owner the following morning – but instead I pulled it out from its hiding place the next evening and carried on reading.

What seemed to me most terrible of all was the fact that everything in the book seemed to be credibly documented. I could disbelieve, I kept persuading myself that I disbelieved, but I could feel my whole world rocking and the ground opening beneath my feet. Who was deceiving me?

Who was telling the truth? Or was it possible for the face of the world to be so imprecise that one person could see in it the features of a Gorgon and another those of Venus? And which face would I find?

The tram stopped at the Libeň Bridge. Suddenly – I was unable to say what force had snatched me out of my self-pitying reverie – I had to glance up towards the exit. All I saw there was a strange girl but there was no doubt that it was she who'd roused me. Something was emanating from her, pressing against me, though she wasn't even looking at me; she wasn't looking at any of the people in the tramcar. There was an absent air about her rather wide and smiling features. She held out a fistful of small change to the conductor, shoved her ticket into the little pocket of her blood-red blouse and sat down. With a gentle movement of her slender fingers she smoothed her sunflower-patterned skirt on her knees, pulled a book from her bag and began to read. I immediately recognized the book: for many years I had drawn from it my knowledge of the history of Czech literature. Just before our school-leaving exams they forbade us to use it; it suffered from bourgeois objectivism, they said, but none of us understood what that meant.

I had never before in my life addressed a strange woman. My past love affairs had begun by my being addressed. But this time I summoned up all my courage. 'You're studying literature too?' I bent down over her, so she should realize I was speaking to her.

She didn't even move her head.

Her refusal to notice me crushed me and my resolution was ebbing away. 'This isn't a good textbook,' I informed her softly, passing on someone else's opinion.

She turned a page and soundlessly moved her wide lips. First she turned to the window, as if to make sure where we'd got to, and then she said: 'You know a better one?'

I could get her any number of textbooks if she was interested. Was she a student of literature?

No, she wasn't a student of literature, she was just interested in it.

A fine interest!

Silence. She was reading again. Her lips were moving. The way she held her head seemed to me distinguished.

I suggested the little area in front of the Rieger monument as the spot where I'd bring her some suitable textbooks at eight the following evening.

Silence. Better that than refusal.

She snapped the book shut. She had it in a leather cover; on the front board I could see a fish embroidered in green and blue beads.

The tram braked at the stop in front of the railway station.

She slipped the book into her bag and walked past me as if I weren't there. I caught up with her at the exit. 'Be sure to come. I'll be waiting for you!' I shoved my wilted carnations into her hand.

'Not that!' she said and got off.

At home I continued reading the typescript. The author listed the posts of those who had been sentenced and executed for treason, counter-revolutionary activity and espionage. They included the leading politicians of the country: the head of the government, his deputies, the chief of the general staff, the highest commanders of the military regions, ambassadors, the president of the Communist International, former chiefs of the secret police. How could a state exist, how could it survive a single day, the author asked, if it was governed by so many traitors? Was it more likely for hundreds or indeed thousands of leading figures of a country to put on a false front for years and commit treason, or for one of them to seize power violently, falsely accuse the others and force them in a bloody stage show to act out a role in which they revile themselves before going to their death?

The paper had a sickly smell of gas. If what was written here was true, how was it that the man was allowed to remain in power in a country that was surely governed by the people? Or wasn't that true either? How could he have led victorious armies? Or didn't he lead them? And why did millions of people cheer him through the years?

Would I ever find out even about events that occurred in my lifetime? So what hope did I have of discovering the truth about events in the distant past? Did Jesus really live, did he perform his miracles, and did he rise from the dead on the third day? Did Moses really converse with God? And anyway, how did the world, which some maintained was created by God's will and others from cosmic vapours, come into being?

But what sense was there in living in a world in which it was impossible to find out the truth about anything?

I arrived early in Rieger Park. Thunderclouds were gathering in the sky and the clank of shunting railway wagons came from the nearby station. I leaned against the trunk of some semi-tropical tree and waited. I'd found several suitable books at home but had brought with me only the *Outline of the History of Literature*. ('*With his class approach the poet sees the nation divided into two classes: on the one hand the bourgeoisie rushing towards its inevitable end, on the other the working class whose strength is increasing with solidarity and to whom belongs the future.*')

I had mentally prepared myself for my date. Although I knew nothing of the girl I was waiting for I assumed that, if she turned up at all and thus gave me some of her time, she would expect some help from me, probably a systematical exposé of the questions she was reading about.

Fortunately I knew my way around literature a bit; I had read, as I now realized, a lot of books and so far I'd had no opportunity to talk about them systematically. Any more than about my life or my opinions. I was full of words like an over-ripe ear of corn: I only had to shake my head a little and they would pour out of me with a quiet rustle.

Just as the first raindrops were beginning to fall I caught sight of her. Colourful as an Amazonian parrot she rose among the flowering shrubs.

'You've really brought the books then?' she breathed a violet exhalation over me that outsmelled the nearby rose bed. She was a little late but that was her boss's fault, a revolting little jerk. First he'd dictated to her some blah-blah for the minister and then he'd pestered her to have dinner with him. Men were a nuisance, they all believed they were the most entertaining company for a lady and all the time were about as entertaining as a goldfish in a bowl. And besides, they were always only out for one thing.

The wind was billowing her skirt and blowing her hair about, her bare arms were glistening. I hadn't allowed for rain in my plans for the evening. So where were we to go?

We hurried down the wet road to the tram stop. At the corner I noticed a blue neon sign. How about sitting in that wine bar for a while?

The air inside was a dark pinkish colour, full of smoke and strange smells. A waiter appeared at our side and led us to an empty table in the darkest corner of the room.

I was trembling with embarrassment and doubts – I knew that my finances would be just about adequate for the university canteen. But my companion seemed satisfied. She opened the folder with the wine list and for a while moved her lips soundlessly.

I ordered wine for her and mineral water for myself. Did she come to places like this often?

Oh yes. Seeing as how her ex-husband used to play the saxophone in the Adriatic bar.

This simple statement took my breath away. I'd been brought up in a mixture of Protestant and revolutionary puritanism. Neither had any time for divorced women.

Fortunately the waiter brought our drinks and she lavished a smile on me. She gripped the stem of her glass and said her name was Vlasta, and from that bastard who'd nearly ruined her life she'd got her ridiculous surname – Slepičková, or Little Hen.

While I was introducing myself she moistened her red lips in her blood-coloured drink and lit a cigarette. Slepička had been the biggest bastard she'd ever known, a liar and a drunk. For a whole six months he'd made her believe that on Saturdays he was playing at funerals and weddings, and she'd sit at home like some widow, and now and then he'd even conjured up some leftovers, and it had been ages before she'd found out that he was simply going to that dive 'Na Slupi' to play bloody cards! When she'd found him there in a tiny backroom behind the bar, one of the chaps, the manager of the firm making Armanda boot polish, was just raking in at least fifty grand. But she'd raised such a shindy that the manager grabbed a fistful of notes, stuffed them into her handbag and begged her, 'Do calm down, please, dear Vlasta, come, how about a smile'! Slepička hadn't said a single word to her, sometimes she'd thought he was round the bend, like when he assured her that he'd spent the whole afternoon with their friend Max when all the time she'd been sitting with dear Max in the Šroubek bar. Can't live with a chap like that, she'd sooner live with a blind man or a cripple. So would I please register that she could put up with anything except lies and pretence.

Same goes for me, I said, I couldn't see myself living with anyone who told lies. I'd always longed for sincerity, I'd never deceived anyone and never would.

She smiled. She'd heard such pretty words before, many times. But she'd like to believe me. She only hoped I wasn't some kind of artist. What did I actually do?

Although a moment earlier I'd talked of sincerity I dared not admit my real ambitions to her, so I said I was studying Czech language and literature.

She'd once known someone who studied architecture, maybe I knew him too, his name was Borek.

No, I didn't know any Borek who was a student of architecture. Sorry.

Well, he hadn't been a student for some time. Five years ago he'd set up on his own, then they'd locked him up, I could probably imagine what kind of cove he was if he ended up like that. But he'd been a divine dancer. Just like a mountaineer she'd known, his name had been Peter – Peter Hrobář, in case I happened to know him – he'd danced like Sasha Machov, he was forever inviting her to go to the Tatra mountains with him, he'd teach her rock climbing and abseiling and glissading in the snow with an icepick, except that by then she'd been married and Slepička would have made mincemeat of her if he'd as much as caught a glimpse of her with another bloke. Actually, she'd been lucky because that guy Hrobář had got himself buried under an avalanche and when they'd dug him out his pick was pushed into his stomach right up to the shaft, and what sport did I go in for?

She finished her glass and the obsequious waiter instantly offered her another.

Then she told me about her father. He'd been an officer. He'd had about ten receivers and a transmitter in the house, and that had finally cost him his head because right through the war he'd never stopped transmitting. She could still see them bursting in early one morning, before daybreak even, bloody swine, but she'd better spare me the details because I looked to her like a chap with a weak constitution. After the war her mother had found a lover for herself, man called Horák, got a job as national administrator in some expropriated factory in Karlovy Vary, maybe I knew him. When they got married they lived in a villa with its own pond for a couple of years, except that – and I'd probably experienced the same sort of thing – the works council turned up one day and moved them out with their own hands. He'd done time for twelve years. But by then they were living in Loket, they had a room in a former cowshed and mum was doing the milking. Then one Sunday she put on her best togs and said she was off to find out who was living in their villa. They'd been searching for her for five days before they fished her out of the pond behind the villa. That was some parting, she could tell me, but she wouldn't go into details of how she'd gone on when they'd shown her her mother. So she was left on her own. She'd always been a decent dancer and so she thought they might take her on in some bar, except that at the time they were closing down those joints because they weren't the right entertainment for Stakhanovites. No job to be found anywhere, and just then she'd run across that man Slepička in Prague. If I saw him I'd probably be surprised. Ugly mug, bald, nearly twenty years older than her, and if she hadn't been so broke and all alone in the world she wouldn't have sat down at the same table with him. Anyway, she'd not been able to stand him even for a year and she'd made the last few months real hell for him. And then one day, when he'd gone off to that bar of his, she'd invited round a chum with whom she'd worked in the factory, they'd bundled Slepička's things into a suitcase and chucked it outside the door, and then they'd changed the lock. The chum had then preferred to stay with her on the inside in case Slepička cut up rough. And he did too, she'd rather not tell me about it or I might get nightmares.

After I'd settled the bill I was left with two three-crown notes and a handful of change. The outside world smelled of damp and dissolved soot. My companion took long strides on her high heels and kept waving from a distance at any passer-by coming our way.

She lived at the top end of Libeň, at the corner of a street that consisted only of a few tenement blocks, and she said this was where she lived and I needn't come along any further, people would only see us and I knew what people were like. How long could she keep my book?

As long as she needed it. Indeed I could get her others and more interesting ones.

We arranged that I'd bring them along to her in a week's time. She gave me her hand, I squeezed it and then, obeying a voice that told me I wouldn't be entirely rejected, I embraced her.

Her lips were moist and sweet as they pressed against mine. But immediately she pushed me back. 'Now not that! That's not what we agreed!'

On my table at home, under a reproachful note from my mother ('It's midnight and you're still loafing about somewhere!') I found a letter from my father from prison. It was written on a lined sheet of octavo, with a circular, purple rubber stamp at the top, right next to the opening words.

My dears,

I am sure you can appreciate that I have enough time here to reflect on my entire past life, on all my aspirations and also on the mistakes I committed. But my biggest mistake was that I observed everything around me as if from the outside. From the outside everything looks simpler and often also more alluring, but a man can be terribly wrong in his judgement, that's something I've only come to realize here. I often think now of my own father: I was about ten when he gave me a microscope for Christmas. He advised me to put a drop of coloured water on a slide and he asked what I thought it would look like. I replied that it would be pure and clear. I had no idea that that pure water would be so full of life. To this day I remember the multitude of amazing movement. A pity my father died when I was still young; he couldn't pass on to me any of his wisdom. I blame myself that, although fate granted me to be with you for a lengthy period, I was probably never wise enough to explain to you that so many things appear different from what they are in reality, and in my mind I ask for your forgiveness . . .

I visualized my father lying in a cell somewhere while I was drifting about wine bars with a strange dolled-up divorcee. All week long, I decided, I would have only dry bread for breakfast, I'd bring it home from the canteen. And I wouldn't meet her again, I didn't want to see her ever again, she was no woman for me.

When at last I lay down and closed my eyes I saw the sea. My visions before falling asleep always came from my childhood. They would emerge unexpectedly and they would stay with me for a while, long enough to inspect them in detail. Sometimes they were so striking, colourful or so bizarre that they stayed in my memory long after they'd vanished. Mostly I wouldn't reflect on their meaning, I just enjoyed them as they were. But, three days before they dragged us off from home during the war, I'd seen a long train with huge wheels. It was moving through a waste land that looked dead. The waste land was still, and full of stones, dried shrubs and straw-like grass, but the gigantic wheels were turning, and I felt a sense of horror. Similarly, the night before our neighbour in the block turned on her gas tap, I'd also seen a rocky landscape with snakes peeping out from under the boulders. At the centre, on a boulder, lay a woman with a rattlesnake eating into her leg. Its eyes were sulphur-yellow, its head was black and it had large poisonous fangs.

But now I was seeing the sea. The waves were washing over me from all sides, so I must have been somewhere in the middle of the water, I was lying on a sun-warmed rock and below the surface I caught sight of a strange fish which looked almost human. Its body was covered with large, plate-like scales, giving it the appearance of a dragon. I noticed that welling up from the fish's flashing eyes were glassy, rainbow-coloured tears which soon dissolved in the water.

The following week, in addition to a translation of a *Soviet Theory of Literature* ('*We define literature as one of the forms of ideology, as a specific form of reflection of life, and we are thereby laying down the basis of its evaluation*'), I brought along to our date Engels's *Origin of the Family and the State* ('*The first class conflict which emerges in history coincides with the development of the antagonism between husband and wife in monogamous marriage and the first class oppression is the oppression of the female sex by the male sex*'), probably in order to prove my liberal attitude to women.

We walked together down a deserted path along a dead arm of the Vltava and I learned that her mother's brother Robert had left home when he was fourteen and had gone to

America, where he became a sailor on the *President Lincoln* and rose as high as First Officer. In the war in the Pacific he'd been captured by the Japanese who'd forced him to build the bridge on the River Kwai. After the war he'd been decorated, the President himself had received him and given him some Order of the Lion or the Eagle, but last year poor Uncle Robert had driven over a mine in Korea, leaving a wife and five children.

Her family with a hero on the wrong side made me uneasy, although at the same time I was touched by her apparent trust in me. Then, at her request, we dropped into some dingy bar that was full of gipsies and strange characters whom she greeted like old friends.

That gipsy over there with the inflamed eyes, yes that one, but I'd better not look at him – she pointed him out to me when we'd ordered some beer – that was no ordinary gipsy fiddler. He'd had his own band and during the currency reform he'd dragged a whole potato-sack full of banknotes up to the counter, money the people would stick to his forehead as he played in the bar, but when he realized what they wanted to change it for, she'd rather not tell me what he'd said to them. Anyway, they'd dragged him off in handcuffs but after two months they'd kicked him out again, probably because they didn't have enough room inside. Ever since, he'd been hanging around here. And my companion directed a friendly smile at that unshaven, scarred chap with his bloodshot eyes and added that he'd once got into a fight over her with some carter who used to be a fairground boxer, Standa Růžička his name was. Admittedly, Standa first broke his nose for him and dislocated his left hand but the gipsy had then brought out his flick-knife and Standa was carted off in an ambulance.

We ordered some goulash and she allowed me to call her by her first name.

I saw her to the corner of the street where she lived and there began to kiss her. She freed herself only after a while.

'But, pet,' she addressed me reprovingly, 'ain't you in too much of a hurry?'

It was getting on for midnight when I reached the tram stop, my mood hadn't quite evaporated but beneath my contentment lurked an uneasy feeling. Something wasn't right, something more serious than that I'd been drinking beer, sitting in a pub and spending money which was supposed to be for my keep. A short while ago I'd been kissing a woman I didn't know. What I knew was a mere handful of words which didn't add up. Could one get close to someone who was covered in words like fish-scales?

The typescript still smelled of gas. Fortunately I'd only a few more pages to read.

The dichotomy of Stalin's character and his role emerge more clearly if we compare him with his ill-famed contemporary, Hitler.

Now that was really going too far. I hesitated. But then I gave way to a dizzy, trembling delight.

The similarities are numerous and stunning. Both ruthlessly crushed and murdered their opponents. Both built up a police apparatus of a totalitarian state and subjected the people to its lasting and murderous pressure. Both tried to change the thinking of their nations, to give them another shape, one that would rule out any undesirable stimulus or influence. Both declared themselves irremovable rulers and governed in the spirit of a rigid Führer principle . . .

I shut my eyes.

> Far better that false hope should lull you
> Than that sheer blackness yawn at you . . .

For my next date I took with me an essay on contemporary Western literature. ('*As though from a pack of jackals there came a howl in unison from bourgeois pseudo-scholars, media tycoons and theorizing crows decked out in professorial gowns. In the USA, that hotbed of imperialism, the gunmen's violence against all culture is being whipped up to probably unprecedented heights . . . ')*

It was a rainy evening again. But she came running along in a short-sleeved blouse and in patent-leather pumps. She didn't feel like drifting around anywhere, so if I didn't mind we could sit about in her place, only for a while, mind you, because she was really all in, she'd had a hellish day, and if it weren't that she'd promised to come she'd have said to hell with it all and gone straight to bed.

She lived on the ground floor. We passed a number of doors, it didn't really look like a residential block, more like doors into offices or into hotel rooms. She unlocked the last one. We passed through a tiny hall with a tap over a chipped sink. Her room was minute – squeezed into it were a convertible couch, a little table with chairs and a single-door wardrobe. Above the couch rose an angel keeping a curly-headed schoolboy from falling off a narrow footbridge into the raging waters below. Dirty, yellowed net-curtains covered a barred window. Leaning against the side of a small radio set were a few books. Among them I spotted my *Origin of the Family* and a *Textbook of Physics* for the Lower Forms of Secondary Schools.

I had carefully prepared a number of questions for the evening but now I asked her in surprise if she was also interested in physics. She replied that she was interested in everything. She sat down on the couch which was bluish-green like the water above which the angel hovered and said she'd also read the book I'd brought her last time, how those Indians all slept together, a lot of nonsense really, probably all thought up by some dirty old man who could only dream of these things nowadays.

This approach to a classic which was universally revered so confused me that I was unable to start a conversation about the book, even though a number of my questions were intended to arise from just that text (what were her views on God, on materialism and on marriage?).

So I asked her out of the blue if she still went dancing.

Not for a long time!

As a matter of fact, she hadn't ever told me what she did.

She hadn't told me? She was surprised. Didn't she say she was in the secretarial department of that dwarf?

But I didn't even know who that dwarf was!

A lot of people were showing a lot of interest lately in what she did. If I really wanted to know what they were manufacturing at her factory there was no reason why she shouldn't tell me, but I didn't look as if I'd be interested when I was reading books about who some savage children called Mummy and who they called Auntie. She'd rather show me what she looked like when she'd got married.

From the wardrobe she dug out an album from the black cover of which shone a red heart overlaid with mica.

I sat next to her and stared at a mass of strange figures and at her own ordinary face – frozen in perpetuity. She was sitting so close to me that I forgot all my questions and put my arms round her.

For a while we rolled about wildly on the bluish-green couch under the unconcerned eyes of the angel. Then she stood up and put the album away. She didn't want to turf me out but she was really tired. If only the next day were Sunday.

But there were three whole days till Saturday!

She yawned. All right, I could come then if I felt like it.

The next day I took the typescript back to my friend. I was prepared to point out to him my doubts about the author's impartiality and in my heart I hoped that my friend – even though he couldn't have known any more than I did what things had really been like – would agree with me.

But he replied that everything that had happened was just one more horrifying episode in an eternally repeated pattern of history. History repeated itself because man ceaselessly desired immortality, the power of creation. He wanted to be like God, yet he was created from the dust of the earth and forever condemned to it. Whoever wished to create new worlds and break out of the mortal order invariably only shed blood. The more a person rebelled and endeavoured to be like God the more fanatically he would be working towards ruin. That was the law of history. Very possibly the next person to declare himself God would complete death's work and leave behind him a planet laid waste.

I was depressed when I left him. What was there left to believe in, and whom to believe?

Before falling asleep I thought of her. I was touching her warm arms and unbuttoning her dress until her magnificent breasts popped out before my eyes and I could cup them in my hands.

Suddenly I saw a waste land. Waves of sand ran across an endless plain, and the wind sucked up the finest grains and carried them ahead like a transparent veil. Outlined against the distant horizon were bare, waterless jagged teeth of rocks. Then I noticed how, from under a nearby dune, the familiar head of the great leader was emerging. Hair brushed back above a pockmarked forehead, under his big nose a huge moustache covering the entire upper lip. On his right shoulder the man was carrying an oblong object. As he approached I could make out not only the features of his face but also the shape of the object. It was a coffin.

On Saturday morning I chose a green silk square in a little shop on Marshal Stalin Street. In each corner of the silk square sat a white dove, evidently designed to symbolize peace but to me it suggested love. When I was told the price I hesitated for a moment, but the assistant said I'd made a good choice and that the girl (or maybe my mum?) would be delighted with it, and so – sentenced to another week of dry bread for breakfast – left with the little package prettily done up with paper ribbon.

She was pleased with the square and, immediately saying that she had something for me too, she produced from the wardrobe a bottle of clear transparent liquid. She fetched two little glasses and I, even though I'd never drunk anything stronger than beer and remembering that alcohol was a poison that dulled man's wit and turned him into a beast, gratefully accepted her gift.

The drink smelled of aniseed and rapidly went to my head, and, as I looked at her, it occurred to me that it didn't really matter how well I knew her or how much I knew about her, what mattered was what I felt and that I desired her.

I began to talk about myself. After all, I hadn't told her much about myself, in fact I hadn't even mentioned my greatest experience: four years – or nearly four whole years – during the war compulsorily spent in the ghetto on the banks of the Ohře river. One day, along with some friends, I'd crept out on to the ramparts where there were ripe cherries on the trees. To climb up on the ramparts was forbidden, but we were hungry and hadn't had any fruit for several years. We were about to return with our booty in our pockets and were running down the slope when the most brutal of the SS guards, a man called Heindel but the name doesn't matter, appeared on his chestnut horse. We could have tried to run, but suppose he started firing at us? But, if he caught us and found out our names, that would mean deportation to Poland, and although we knew nothing then about gas chambers we knew that the journey meant something terrible. Anyway it was too late to run away, the horse was moving at a fast trot and in the few seconds we'd hesitated he'd caught up with us. We ducked of course but the rider stood in his stirrups and cracked his whip several times across our faces. I'd just about managed to cover my face but one of my friends had a bloody gash on his cheeks and lip. Actually we heaved a sigh of relief, we were glad it wasn't anything worse than the whip. I could tell her quite a few incidents like this but I didn't want to, I'd merely tried to explain to her the origin of my anxieties about the world, of the unease that had remained with me ever since. Armed men on horseback frequently rode through my dreams and saw to it that I didn't forget my defencelessness. I wanted her to understand the scars on my soul, even though I disliked the word soul because – I didn't know how she felt about it – I didn't really believe in it. I'd known too many people who could have had a soul but had less of it than some dog, horse or even wolf, and also, unfortunately, I found myself unable to believe in immortality or to believe that one day I'd meet again all those whom I'd been fond of and who had been killed. I believed only in life, in a short stay on earth, in a single birth and a single death, not even therefore in what, as far as I knew, the Indians believed, in no reward or punishment after death, and in no reincarnation, or continuation. And therefore I realized that if I wanted something I had to work for it now, while I was still alive, before my life drew to its close, so that I might see the results myself. Maybe all this sounded a little confused and mundane, but I certainly wasn't one of those who were just out for that one thing only, I wanted more than that, I wanted something deeper and higher – what was it actually I wanted? Yes, above all I wanted to live as a good, useful and truthful person, achieve something for other people, for mankind, and hence also for her. That's why I'd like to understand her as much as I could, and get to know her, and get close to her. Sometimes I had a feeling that she was hiding from me, that she was talking to draw away from me, but that was no good. Speech should draw people together, that was the gift of language, that it could open instead of close, reveal instead of conceal, language was the greatest invention and, if I believed in God, I'd say that it was his greatest gift to man, but what had I been about to say? Oh yes, I longed for her sincerity, I was sincere to her, too, otherwise I couldn't live, otherwise we'd pass each other like ships in the night. And everybody hoped to leave some trace. What did I mean by that? Had she ever observed those new aeroplanes which flew at colossal altitudes? They pass, they disappear, but they leave a white trail in the sky when they are gone. That was a trace. Or a person crosses a snowfield and disappears. There's no one anywhere, only snow, a wide empty plain, but then a wanderer who's lost his way comes along, and what does he find? Right, a track. And by following it he gets to his destination, or maybe not to his destination but to the one of the person who left the trail, and maybe just there he'll find what he'd been looking for all his life and hadn't hoped ever to find. Maybe some human being was waiting for him there with sad eyes, like hers, or a house, some stone shelter amidst the frosty waste, and that shelter was a salvation, a place of rest. I knew she didn't like artists and I wasn't saying I was an artist, but I'd like her to know what sometimes happened to me: I was gripped by a suspicion, a magnificent and almost frightening suspicion not only about myself but about the world, about the origin of things, a glimpse of the truth, actually only a picture that I had to communicate. It was only a picture, as if disjointed fragments were joining up before my eyes, could she imagine that? They'd only been fragments, meaningless confusion, and now suddenly I saw a picture.

She rose, moved the chair away, reached over to the radio and switched it on. How about a spot of dancing? I didn't know how? Never mind, she'd teach me, she was passionately fond of dancing. She swayed around me, then she picked up the bottle and the two glasses, put them on the chair by the couch, pushed the table over to the wall, and suddenly I was sitting there as if I were naked.

What was I waiting for? She stopped in front of me and extended her arms. So I got up, put my arms round her and for a while tried to stamp my feet in time to the music. She said she'd teach me the steps, she'd used to dance with Borek at the Alfa and in all sorts of night-clubs, I really should see him some time. Any ordinary dancer after a while found his legs getting heavy and his hands sweating, one, two, three, whereas he, the longer he was on the floor, the lighter he seemed to get till his feet seemed to leave the ground, and when everybody else had dropped out he'd ask for a solo for himself and her. But not a waltz or some

Arrow in the Savannah, they'd do the jive till they dropped, and the band, when they'd finished, would always applaud them, one, two, three, couldn't I hear: one, two, three and bring your foot up, or was I really deaf, how could I stamp so out of time?

Fortunately the music stopped and an announcer took over, and halfway through an unsuccessful dancing step, I drew her to me and kissed her.

She said she'd see if there was some other music on. OK, just as I liked. At least she'd put the table back where it belonged. Just as I liked.

We were lying on the couch, the voice on the radio was monotonously reading the news in some Nordic language, and I suspected that the moment was approaching. I kissed her, pressed her to myself; I loved her, I really loved her and that gave me the right. She wasn't a fish, she was a butterfly – a butterfly had scales too, but more beautiful ones than a fish and it wasn't slippery even if it was just as hard to catch. We were still kissing, she had closed her eyes and was breathing rapidly.

I whispered to her that she was beautiful, colourful like a rainbow, like a butterfly from the Orinoco, she had the same eyes, butterfly eyes, eyes like . . .

She asked: 'You want to go to bed already?'

She got up, with skilled movements transformed the couch into a bed, from its inside produced a white sheet and a duvet with a clean cover evidently put on freshly that day. She ordered me to turn round; I could hear the grating noise as she drew the curtains, then the voice which had been solemnly reading the news disappeared, there was a rapid sequence of other voices, then some guitar music and simultaneously the rustling of clothes. It was my turn now to undress. I slipped out of my trousers, the springs of the couch creaked behind me, and I turned round. She was lying with the bedclothes drawn up to her chin – like in a film – and on the chair, in an untidy heap, lay her underwear. Under the bedclothes, then, nakedness was awaiting me, total nakedness that I'd be able to touch – the realization nearly choked me. I ought to take my underpants off but I was embarrassed.

'Why don't you switch off, pet?'

I did as she asked, groped my way to the couch from memory, stripped off the rest of my clothes, and was now ready for my first night of love – at least my body seemed to be ready, but my soul, the one I'd denied a little while earlier, was in a state of embarrassment and uncertainty. Did I love her enough? Was I prepared to love her now for the rest of my life? Make her my wife not just for that one evening? Anyway, would I come up to scratch?

I realized that her fingers were lightly running along my thighs.

'You're trembling all over, pet!'

Surely she mustn't touch me *there*! I shut my eyes, hurriedly performed what I wanted and what she probably expected.

She too, I now noticed, was trembling. She pressed herself against me, as if seeking protection with me.

I was aware of the aniseed odour behind my back, also of the overbearing violet fragrance of her perfume. Suddenly sadness gripped me. I had always believed I'd do this only out of a great and total love. Why hadn't I waited?

She bent over me and kissed me. 'I hope you took precautions, pet! I wouldn't like to find myself in the club again!'

'Again?'

She embraced me.

'You have a child?' I asked.

She reached for the bottle which stood behind her and filled both glasses. 'Don't be so nosy!'

'I was only asking!'

'Curiosity killed the cat!'

I pushed her away and leapt out of bed.

'D'you still see him? Or hear from him?'

She made me sit down on the white sheet again. 'I haven't,' she embraced me. 'Haven't had one for a long time.'

'What happened to it?'

She enveloped me with her warmth and violet perfume. 'Now, now, you don't have to think about it now!' A stranger's warm body was pressing against mine, a stranger's fingers were catching hold of me, entwining me, bewitching me, leading me back to her.

'See, you can be nice, you can be very nice,' she whispered and rolled me over, she treated my body as if it belonged to her already, and I was aware that instead of feeling angry I whispered to her that I loved her, while I was flooded by unexpected waves of renewed pleasure.

This time I didn't close my eyes, I looked at her: her tousled hair was falling over her dewy forehead, on her upper lip too there were some droplets of perspiration, while the right-hand corner of her lower lip was bleeding. I looked at her lips and then at her breasts and I realized that I was free to look at her breasts, that I could touch them, that I could do anything, and I felt vertigo gripping me. Suddenly I felt that there was nothing more important than that she was lying there next to me and I could touch her, I could do anything now, and I began to understand that this was what love was all about, that this was the emotion for which people were prepared to suffer, to hate, to endure injustice, to be impoverished, to go to the end of the world barefoot and to die.

She opened her eyes and for a while gazed lifelessly at the ceiling. Then she said: 'I killed him.'

'Whom?' I gasped.

'Nothing. A gnat!'

'You killed that child?'

Silence. From somewhere, I didn't quite understand where it came from, a rustling moth had appeared and was flitting round the glass bowl of the ceiling light.

She stretched out for her glass. 'But it was a long time ago.'

I was silent, I couldn't think of anything to say.

'Don't be like that, pet. Please don't. You said you loved me.'

It had happened at the end of the war. She'd been snatched out of school and taken to Germany. Strictly speaking it hadn't been Germany but the Sudetenland, as they called it then. She was to work in a factory producing motor fuel and eventually, because she was young and weak, they'd sent her to some old woman on a farm. Six horses, cows and pigs too many to count, and the whole lot run by one old woman and an old man with a detachable wooden leg. Mostly she didn't get to bed till midnight, and at four in the morning the cripple kicked at the door. Only time off was Sunday afternoon. The old woman put on a black dress, picked up a prayer book and shuffled to church. The priest, for his part, had a wooden hand and part of his chin had been shot off, so he looked like the devil himself. He'd preach something she didn't understand but the old woman would howl. Probably she remembered her men-folk, their photos were hanging over her bed: an older man and three young louts – except for one of them they all had black crepe on the frames. The one who was still alive, Johann Sebastian, turned up in uniform just as the harvest began: they'd given him leave. He'd brought some chocolate with him and some raisins which he slipped her, and all the time he'd look at her in a way that made her run away. He chased her everywhere, and then he'd give her some salami and cigarettes, and she was afraid to go to bed at night, she slept in a tiny hole next to the cowhouse and the door couldn't be locked. She'd have waited till he'd gone to bed, except that he came when she'd fallen asleep; she'd have struggled with him but what was the use, he'd only calmly have put a bullet through her. After a week he left and she never heard from him again, but her belly began to swell. It was born in April, she didn't even have time to get it christened, and anyway the priest had taken to his heels like everybody else; only the old woman and that cripple had stayed behind for her sake. They'd forced her to come along with them, they'd take her away on a cart, but she'd skedaddled during the night. She could have left *it* there but

113

she didn't want to do that, anyway *it* would have died, so she took *it* with her.

And then?

Nothing, She'd held a pillow to its little mouth and then she'd left *it* in the forest. Covered *it* up a bit with earth and dry leaves. There were corpses lying about everywhere then. Did I think she shouldn't have done it?

I didn't think anything. My head was in a turmoil, I was tangled up in the sticky threads of her voice, my feet were shaking with weakness. I put on my clothes.

'You're leaving already, pet?'

That was the only thing I longed to do.

'I needn't have told you about it, you know, but I wanted you to know. Seeing you'd slept with me.'

It was a dirty, cold night outside. I'd nearly got to the tram stop when I heard my name called. I froze as if some voice from beyond the grave had spoken to me, as though death itself were calling out to me. She was running after me, she was wearing only her slip and on her legs she had gossamer-thin stockings – nothing else.

'You never even said,' she panted, 'if you'll come again. If you'll ever come again!'

'But I know where you live now.'

'You can't just come whenever you feel like it!'

'I can't?'

'No!'

'Why not?'

'It's impossible. Some dreadful things. I couldn't tell you about them all.' She was standing before me, shivering.

'What couldn't you tell me about?'

'I can't! He'd immediately . . . I can't! Some other time, if you'll come again.'

Why had I wanted to know anything about her? 'Someone else is seeing you?' And I felt a slight touch of jealousy.

She put her hand on my shoulder.

'Shall I come tomorrow?'

'Not tomorrow, that's just it.'

'The day after?'

'Can't be sure. Better not!'

I promised her I'd come on Wednesday evening. She accompanied me to the tram, although I objected that dressed like that she couldn't walk in the street. She kissed me once more, then she ran back home. In her white slip, with her tousled hair flying about her head, she looked like a wraith.

When the tram came I got into the empty trailer. I pressed my forehead against the cold, vibrating plate glass and felt like crying.

At home I looked out a book covered in blue school paper. (*'The new criminal law represents the expression of the political will of the working masses, the expression of the new socialist legality.'*) Since my father's arrest I knew my way about it pretty well. I found it without difficulty. Murder of a newborn child by its mother – if in fact this relatively mild article could still be made to apply to her deed.

I also had to write to my father:

Dear Dad,

First of all thank you for your fine letter and I'd like to assure you that you are mistaken at least in thinking that you'd not passed on to us any of your wisdom and hadn't taught us to look beyond the surface of things and appearances. On the contrary, it always seemed to me that you invariably tried to get to the root of everything (just as you taught me to work out the roots of equations) that might seem insoluble, and that's probably just another name for what I'd call seeking the truth.

I liked my own words, they seemed to me exalted and inspiring.

I too am striving for the same thing, and I have chosen what I want to be chiefly because I want to get as close as possible to the roots of things, and I assure you that

115

everything that has happened to us I accept as a spur to reflect on our past lives.

I wondered for a moment how to fit a report on my present experiences into the letter and then I added:

> Besides, I too am now passing through something of which I cannot at the moment speak in detail because I don't understand it all myself, but it does seem to me like contact with real life . . .

I hesitated over the last sentence, wondering whether I had betrayed too much to those who would be reading the letter even before my father did, but it seemed to me more probable that even he wouldn't understand what I was on about. Maybe it was better that way.

On Wednesday, even before six, I rang her doorbell. In vain. It was only then that I noticed that there was no name on her door. Could I have made a mistake? I rang once more. At the far end of the passage a fat woman in curlers looked out. 'Looking for someone?'

I walked over to her. 'Miss – Mrs Slepičková.'

'Don't know her.' She looked at me for a while as if waiting for some explanation, then she added: 'Doesn't live here!' She tossed her head, which looked like the disconnected inside of some piece of electrical equipment, and again vanished behind her door.

We met at the entrance to the block. Her clothes, as always, glowed colourfully and she was carrying a bunch of flowers. 'Been waiting long, darling?' She kissed me and blew a wine-laden breath over me. 'I didn't think you'd come, thought you wouldn't give a damn for me now.'

'But I promised . . . '

She kissed me again. Then she explained that they'd had a party at work, she'd boozed a bit too, but only a tiny little bit, she was thinking of me, that she had to get home in time in case I came after all, and she'd brought me some of the left-overs because she'd forgotten all about food, I must be starving, poor thing.

In her room the bed was unmade, on the table stood a half-finished bottle of wine and, my heart ached at the sight, two wine glasses.

She'd had a girl friend here last night, she'd turned the radio on, they'd sat talking till after midnight, then she'd dropped into bed and in the morning she'd overslept, no time even to make the bed. From her handbag she produced some sandwiches wrapped in a paper napkin. She told me to help myself and went out into the hall with her flowers. I could hear the water running, and her voice, as she sang quite happily to herself. Everything this voice had just been telling me somehow vanished.

When she returned she was already undressed, with only a towel wrapped round her. 'Why aren't you eating?' She drew the curtains and then we made love.

It was marvellous, so natural and easy I nearly forgot everything I knew about her, but nevertheless I asked. 'You were about to tell me something last time!'

Sure, but now she didn't know if she should. She'd consulted her girl friend last night and she'd thought she shouldn't tell anybody about it.

What girl friend was that?

They'd sung together in cabaret.

I'd no idea she'd sung in cabaret.

That was a long time ago, when she was hardly out of pinafores. Slepička had fixed it. At the Adria.

And why had she given it up?

That was a long story, it had been Max's fault.

I didn't know any Max.

Max was a mate of Horák, a great chap, fought in England during the war, I should see him in his dress uniform with his gold RAF badge on his lapel. He'd had a processed food factory, made pâtés and goulash, but I wasn't to think that he was a butcher, actually he couldn't bear to see blood and one day when he had to kill a rabbit they had to get him a

117

hunting rifle and he shot it from a distance. That's why he'd joined the Air Force in the war.

And what was the connection between Max and her singing?

Well, at the time she was singing with that gipsy she'd pointed out to me, in the Esplanade bar that was, and Maxie – they'd nationalized his factory by then and he'd had his bags all ready packed – was going to beat it and go back to his RAF, well he came and stuck a thousand-crown bill to the gipsy's forehead, said he wanted a farewell waltz. But the gipsy refused, he wasn't supposed to play that kind of song now but he could give him *Proshchay lyubimiy gorod*. Max stuck another thousand to his forehead and she'd whispered to the gipsy that Maxie was her friend and that during the war . . .

At that moment the tinkle of a bell came from the hall and she fell silent, sat up on the bed and, it seemed to me, her eyes widened and froze motionless. 'That's him!' she whispered.

'Who?'

'Quiet!' Her eyes flew to the door. 'Think he heard us?' She tiptoed to the light switch. Darkness! Only the green eye of the radio still shone.

The bell tinkled again. 'You mean the man you wanted to tell me about?' I asked in a whisper.

The floor creaked softly under her feet, then the eye of the radio also went out. I couldn't see anything. I nearly jumped when I felt the touch of her hand. She pressed herself against me. 'He might come to the window.'

The window was closed and the curtain drawn.

'Who is he?'

She put her hand flat on my mouth. In the silence I heard my breathing and hers; from the distance, maybe several courtyards away, came the sound of an accordion. 'Maybe it was a neighbour,' I suggested.

'No, that was him!'

'Who?'

She was trembling. Then she got up to take a peep from the hall. Maybe he was no longer there. He'd gone away. She'd told him that she'd spend the night at a girl friend's. Even so, I must be careful when I went home and keep right out of his way. Because that man was capable of anything.

How could I avoid him if I didn't know what he looked like?

Well, he was a scraggy, fair-haired fellow, with a scar on his right cheek. Over six foot tall, couldn't mistake him.

What was his name?

Never mind his name.

So why wouldn't she tell me?

Because he'd forbidden her to. He'd kill her if he found out she'd squealed on him. But I could call him Karel.

Who was this Karel?

She wished she knew.

How did she get involved with him?

She'd met him in a bar. About a month before she'd met me. He'd been nice to her. Ordered wine for her, a whole bottle, then he'd taken her home by taxi.

Had she been seeing him?

She couldn't have known she was going to meet me.

Was she still seeing him?

She didn't want to but I just couldn't imagine how scared she was of him.

Why was she so scared?

But he was a murderer. During the war – but that's just what she mustn't talk about.

What happened during the war?

He'd been in the SS.

How did she find out?

He'd told her. She'd also seen his tattoo.

I felt myself going rigid with horror. Or perhaps with the hideousness of it. How did she converse with him when she didn't speak German?

Well, Czech of course. He spoke it so well you wouldn't know who he was. And he'd nice manners. When he visited her he brought her tulips.

119

And after she'd found out what kind of man he was, she still asked him here?

She didn't ask him, he came anyway. Merely told her when to expect him.

'And you wait for him?'

'Once I ran away but he caught me. Then he beat me up. Said, if I did it again, they'd make mincemeat of me.'

'Who?'

'There're several of them!' She was trembling all over.

I embraced her and she kissed me on my mouth.

'Wait a moment, tell me one more thing: He wants something from you?'

'How did you find out?'

'What does he want?'

'That I can't, that I really can't . . .'

'You must tell me everything!'

'No, that I can't.' She burst into tears.

There was no point in tears. She needn't be afraid, we were sure to think of something, only I had to know the truth about what he wanted from her.

She was still sobbing.

Was she going to tell me?

Very well then. But I had to swear I wouldn't breathe a word to anyone.

I was not going to swear in advance. But I wouldn't do anything that might hurt her.

If I grassed on them, they'd find me sure as fate. I'd better be warned. It would be healthier for me not to know anything.

Sure. But it was too late for that now.

She began to kiss me.

'Are you going to tell me?'

She stiffened. For a while she gazed at me intently, then she said, in the same tone she'd use for telling me that he'd asked to get her a packet of cigarettes: 'He wants me to draw him a plan of the factory shop where I work.'

'That's what he wanted?'

'That's what he wants,' she corrected me.

'I thought you worked in the manager's office.'

'Got a good memory, pet! But to him I said I was a shop-floor worker. A fork-lift driver.' She smiled at me coquettishly.

'Why d'you tell him that?'

'I just told him. Maybe because I didn't like him.'

'But you said you'd liked him. To begin with, anyway.'

It was always the same. I peeled away some scales and new ones appeared underneath. I felt like screaming. Or begging. I'd get down on my knees and beg her to tell me how everything really was.

Yes, she'd liked him. And he'd brought her tulips. But he had cold eyes like a crow. When he looked at her, her legs trembled.

And what did she say to him when he told her what he wanted?

What could she say to him when he looked at her like that? That she wasn't sure she could manage it. But he'd said he'd collect it the day after tomorrow. And he'd come today. Maybe he'd got wind that I was here with her.

How would he get that idea – or had she told him about me?

Did I think she was off her rocker?

I didn't think anything nasty about her. But she had told me about him, hadn't she?

Not the same thing, surely?

Indeed not. She mustn't be angry with me, I was a little . . . I'd never been in this kind of situation before.

Did I think she had?

So how could he have got wind that I was here?

They might have a tail on her. They might want to find out whether she had decided to squeal on them.

It wasn't nice of her not to have told me about all that before, not to have mentioned him.

She hadn't wanted to worry me.

Thank you very much. So what was she going to do now? Surely she wasn't going to draw that plan!

So what was she to do? I didn't know him, I couldn't imagine the kind of beast he was. He'd never beaten me up. He'd never told me how he used to shoot Jews.

He'd told her that?

Several hundreds of them he'd shot.

Surely nobody spoke about such things nowadays.

Maybe he'd just wanted to scare her, she hadn't been there. But she knew that if she grassed on him she couldn't expect any kidglove treatment.

But surely she couldn't . . . For that kind of person . . .

Yes, now she realized she couldn't. But did I expect her to run to the people who'd done for her mother and stepfather? She put her arms round me. She was unhappy. She didn't think she had the strength to go on living. She was no longer surprised at her mother. She at least was happy now, at rest.

I promised her I'd think of something by the next day. We agreed to meet outside the Sokol club-house the next afternoon. Then I left.

At home, even though it was past midnight, I pulled out the book in the blue paper and turned the pages till I found my article.

Any person learning in a credible manner that another person intends to commit, or has committed, high treason (Art. 78), conspiracy against the Republic (Arts. 79 and 80), sabotage (Arts. 84 and 85), espionage (Arts. 86 and 87), endangering a state secret . . . and deliberately failing to report such a criminal act immediately to the Prosecutor or to an officer of National Security shall be punished by a term of imprisonment of from one to five years.

At that moment I owed my freedom to a benign fate, to the fact that we had not yet been discovered. Anyway, who would believe in my innocence?

In despair I escaped to my ocean waves. They isolated me from all continents, from all words, laws and acts. On a sun-warmed rock I waited for the shining eyes of my fish to appear. They rose up from the deep, they broke the surface, and behind them a long scaly body emerged. I watched in amazement as those scales, shimmering with all the colours of the rainbow, changed into gossamer-fine feathers, and the fish rose higher above the dark mass of the waters, and it was no longer a fish but a bird of paradise with gentle features, and in its beak glistened a golden ring. I followed it upwards with my eyes and, when it had become a mere dissolving point, I could see it drop the glistening object from high up and I held out my open hands just in time to catch it. I placed the golden ring on my forehead and noticed its delicious, honeyed smell. I lay in the splashing waters, the fish had disappeared and the bird had been swallowed up by the vastness of the sky; all that remained was quiet, warmth and the delicate smell. Only after a while did I sit up, remove from my forehead a dandelion clock, blow at it and watch the silvery fluff rise above the waves. At that moment I realized with clairvoyant certainty that none of the things that filled me with fear were real, that none of it concerned me, that I need not worry, and that I could look forward to the next day.

Outside the Sokol building in the afternoon I could see her colours shining brilliantly from far off, and she smiled at me. Could she smile in that carefree manner if even part of what she'd told me was the truth?

She hadn't heard from that man?

What man?

The one she'd told me about!

But he wasn't supposed to come till the next day!

Again I felt everything come rushing up towards me. She hadn't drawn that plan for him?

Not yet. Surely I'd told her not to give him anything, or had I changed my mind?

I hadn't changed my mind. I'd just like to . . . I had an idea.

Something to eat?

No, it had nothing to do with food. Could we go to her place?

We bought some potato salad, hamburgers and four bottles of beer.

Her room was stuffy and unaired. She switched on the radio, opened the window and got ready to fix the food. I reached across to the radio and turned the volume down. 'How about playing a game?'

'A game?' She tipped the salad onto a plate and sounded suspicious. 'Slepička tried to teach me *mariáš* but I was too dumb.'

'This is a different game.'

She opened a bottle and poured the beer into two glasses. 'Want to go to bed already?'

'Wait! That game – I'd like to explain it to you.'

'But I haven't got any cards here. Slepička took them away with him.'

'This game isn't played with cards.'

'Once we played with matchboxes. But it ended with a lot of filthy language.'

'You don't play this with anything. All you do is talk, and the joke of it is that you've got to tell the truth. Each one may ask the other ten questions.'

'What sort of questions?'

'Any sort you like. You can ask whatever you wish. And I've got to answer you truthfully.'

'I don't know that I'll be able to play it.'

'Why not?'

'Learning all those questions!'

'But you can ask whatever comes into your head.'

'And who wins?'

'Nobody wins. This game isn't about winning.'

'So why d'you play it?'

'For the fun of it.'

'Ten questions is too much!' she objected. 'And you don't have to give forfeits?'

I said that no forfeits need be given and that ten questions was about the right number.

'All right!' She drained her glass and unbuttoned her

blouse so that I could almost see her breasts. She sat down opposite me and crossed her legs. I proposed that she should ask her questions first, but she declined; I'd have to show her how the game was played.

'When did you first get to Germany?' I asked.

'In the spring of forty-four.' She exhibited concentration. As if she were expecting some ambush. Some blow.

'Now you!'

'What, me?'

'Your turn to ask!'

'That was all?'

'All for the moment.'

'I don't understand this. Probably still haven't got the hang of this game.'

'Ask a question then!'

'What's the capital of Turkey?'

'Ankara. But you should ask some question that concerns me.'

'You look like a Turk,' she explained.

'What was the name of the village where you worked on that farm?'

'Wait a minute!' She wrinkled her forehead. 'Armsdorf. I was terrified I mightn't remember. That's all?'

'That's all. Your turn!'

She looked about the room. 'What's your favourite food?'

'Potato dumplings. Dumplings filled with smoked meat and with chopped onions on top.'

'You're not very demanding in your tastes,' she remarked. 'Slepička loved goose liver with almonds or stuffed pigeons. Sometimes he wouldn't bother from morning till midnight and then it would suddenly hit him and he'd devour three steaks right in the kitchen; he used to get them without coupons. Would you like me to make those dumplings for you some time?'

I shrugged. I didn't want to be diverted. I'd thought my questions out carefully. I began with inconspicuous ones and gradually worked towards the ones I considered crucial.

'Who hurt you most in your life?'

'Slepička,' she answered without hesitation. 'All but killed me. More than once.'

'Your turn,' I reminded her. The fact that she didn't mention the German soldier might mean she'd invented him. Or it could mean that anything more remote in time seemed of less importance to her. But why didn't she think of the man who was blackmailing her, threatening her and who had actually beaten her?

'What's your favourite occupation?'

'Writing,' I said.

'You write?'

'Yes.'

'You're a scream!'

'What was the name of the chap who wanted that plan from you?'

'But I've told you: Karel!'

'And what else? Karel can't be his full name!'

'I don't know the rest, he never told me.'

'Come on, he must have told you his name. You can't say you don't know if you do know, otherwise the whole game would be pointless.'

'I don't know,' she repeated. 'If I don't know then I don't know.'

'Last time you said you weren't allowed to tell me. That he forbade you.'

'He forbade me to mention Karel.'

'And he didn't tell you his surname?'

'He didn't tell me anything!'

'And you didn't ask him?'

'Why should I? Didn't ask you yours either.'

'But I told you mine!'

'Anyway, I've forgotten it already.'

'All right. Your turn.'

'What's your favourite drink?'

'Cocoa.'

'You are a scream,' she said. 'A chap whose favourite drink is cocoa!'

'Did you make love with him?'

'Some questions you're asking!'

'You can ask the same kind!'

'I don't care who you screw with. But no!'

'What, no?'

'There was nothing between us. He's sick.'

'How, sick?'

'It's my turn now.'

'I'm sorry,' I said, 'that wasn't meant to be another question.'

'It's from the war. He can't do it – have children. Can I ask my question now? What's your favourite song?'

'I don't really know.'

'Sing one then. One you like.'

'But I can't sing.'

'You never sing? You're a queer fish.'

'It isn't that, but I sing out of tune.'

'Never mind, so you sing out of tune.'

'No,' I said, 'not that!'

'But you've got to, you said so yourself.'

'I said truthfully that I couldn't sing.'

'You're making excuses.'

'I'm not making excuses! Can I go on?'

'As you like.' She leaned over to me and let me kiss her. 'If it still amuses you. Anyway, you're making excuses. I should ask you for a forfeit!'

'What did he offer you for it?'

'Who for what?'

'You know very well!'

'How d'you know he offered me anything?'

'I'm asking the questions.'

She heaved an audible sigh, then she got up, opened her wardrobe, for a while scrabbled about among some clothes, and then fished out a small box. She shoved it right up under my eyes and then lifted the lid.

On a faded, pink cushion lay a ring with a large, sky-blue stone. I knew nothing about jewellery but I could tell the ring was not new.

'That's what he gave me. And he said I'd get another one like it. Afterwards.'

I felt an overwhelming despair – not at her simple-minded openness but at my helplessness, my hopeless uncertainty. I'd never get to the truth – about her, about that man, about this ring. Had it belonged to her grandmother, or her mother, or some murdered Jewess? What was I to do?

'It's beautiful,' she was saying. 'Slepička never gave me a ring, not even for our wedding!' She snapped the box shut and carried it back to the cupboard. Then she poured us out some beer and asked: 'Do we go on playing?'

'We've only had six questions.'

She leaned over to me and kissed me. 'Why did you invent this silly game for me, pet?'

I shrugged. 'I like playing games. Your turn to ask.'

'But I am asking.'

'That was a question?'

'Why not? You wanted to find out something I'm keeping from you, didn't you? You wanted to know if I'd slept with him, didn't you? And with whoever else. Otherwise why think up those dirty questions?'

I probably blushed. 'That's not so!'

She kissed me again. I embraced her.

When we were already lying naked next to each other I said: 'All I wanted to know was whether you hadn't invented it all. That man who wants you to draw the plan for him. That SS man.'

She pressed her whole body against me.

'I beg you, tell me the truth.'

'All right!' She tore herself away again. 'What d'you want me to tell you?'

'Was it all as you told me?'

'How else d'you think it was?'

'You swear?'

'What do you mean? What the hell do you mean?'

'Swear to me, I beg you! Do this one thing for me!'

'And what else do you expect? You come here, you get between my sheets, then you think up some questions I'd be ashamed to repeat. Who do you think you are? You can stuff your questions!'

I tried to get up but she started kissing me. Then we dressed and went into town. We found the district police station and I told her I'd be waiting for her in the bar opposite. First I saw her to the enquiries counter.

At the bar I ordered frankfurters with mustard and a bottle of mineral water. Time dragged on as it does in a dentist's waiting room. Suppose they said she'd been rather slow coming to see them, that she'd neglected her duty and they'd keep her inside? And suppose the chap I'd never seen wasn't what he said at all but just an ordinary madman?

What could they be questioning her about for so long? Or was she telling them the story of her life, how they'd murdered her father, how her mother had drowned herself and how her uncle had driven over a mine in Korea and pushed his ice-pick into his guts?

Suppose it wasn't that chap who was mad, but she herself? Had she invented everything she was now telling them? The whole story – or was she telling them a different one? Something about me?

But surely she'd seen his tattoo mark. It seemed to me that a person could invent a whole incident but that there were certain details that couldn't be invented, they had to be seen or experienced.

At midnight I had to get out of the bar but I had nowhere to go, so I sat down on the steps outside. In several windows of the building opposite the lights were still on. Those windows had bars across them and the glass was frosted. Behind which of them should I look for her? Or had they already taken her away somewhere?

I thought of my father. Behind what window would he be waiting now? I shut my eyes to fend off a sudden attack of vertigo. The artificial lights were fragmented into rainbow colours between my eyelashes. I was waiting for them to fall into a pattern, I was hoping for my mental picture, for just one cool wave to wash over my dirty step, a wave whose crash would disturb the stuffy silence of this night, but nothing appeared, nothing, nothing, even the last remnants of the rainbow were swallowed up by the darkness. I was lying at the bottom of a shaft, there was no sky left above me. How had I got there? When and how had I stumbled into that place? Would I ever see the light of day again?

In terror I forced myself to open my eyes and there she was standing before me.

I leapt to my feet and she took my arm. I noticed that she was shivering – possibly from cold or fatigue, and possibly from excitement. I wanted her to tell me everything, but she said she didn't feel like it and anyway they'd forbidden her to.

And what about her? About tomorrow? Would they catch him before then?

They hadn't appeared to be anxious to catch him at all. She was to wait for him as if nothing was wrong. How about having a drink somewhere?

Everything would be closed now.

Was that the time? She'd had no idea she'd been so long.

But if he came, surely he'd want that plan from her?

Supposed to let him have it!

That's what they said?

They'd said to act naturally. Give him the plan and anything else he might want! And report to them on everything.

And suppose he found out and did something to her?

They'd promised to protect her. She needn't be afraid.

When we parted outside her block she embraced me almost frantically and said I mustn't for God's sake abandon her now. She was terribly scared, she'd be scared all night and all tomorrow, she'd be scared all the time because, if he saw it in her face, he'd surely kill her. And, if he didn't, then the others would who were in it with him – as soon as they realized who'd shopped them. Why had she listened to me, why had she gone to that place, she should have told me to stuff it, and hadn't he promised that once he had the material he'd get the hell out of here and she'd never hear from him again; she would have been left in peace and, what's more, she'd have another ring, and the way things were now what had she got? I would drop her anyway, she realized that, she could feel it in her bones.

I dried her cheeks with a handkerchief and promised not to leave her but to come and see her again soon, and why not this Sunday.

I was afraid, too. Suppose that unknown person realized that she was playing a double game with him? After all, she only needed a drink and she'd spill the lot to him, she'd warn him: from stupidity, from pity, or in order to get that other ring out of him, she'd even tell him that it was I who'd dragged her *there*, and the villain, whom they would perhaps be shadowing to find out where he went and whom he met, would make straight for me, either to kill me on the spot or deviously to denounce me as his accomplice. Who could help me? Oh Lord.

On Sunday, before entering her building I looked in all directions like a conspirator approaching a clandestine meeting.

I rang the bell but there was no movement inside. I was about to beat a hasty retreat when I noticed the corner of white paper peeping out of her letterbox. In a large, almost childish, hand it said: MISS IVANKA KLÍMOVÁ.

I pulled the note out of the letterbox. It read:

Dear Ivanka,
    First of all lots of love. I'm sorry I had to go suddenly to·
Teplice to see a girl friend. Let me hear from you some time!
    Looking forward to it, Your Vlasta

Where had she really gone off to, and after whom? And that man – was he locked up by now? Or was she escaping from him? And had she told him about me?

Four days later I rode over to her place again, but still there was no reply when I rang the bell. It occurred to me that I might never see her again but that thought produced, if anything, a sense of relief.

And then I began to miss her: her colourful appearance, making love to her, and even her tragic and highly implausible stories. Would I ever find out whether these things had actually taken place? By the end of summer I had tried at least three times to find her in at home. I would have left a note in her letterbox, with my address, but I was afraid that it might fall into the wrong hands. Finally I screwed up my courage and rang the bell at the other end of the passage.

The familiar plump woman opened the door.

Slepičková, Slepičková, she kept repeating, no, she didn't know her, there used to be an odd person living there, named, now what was her name? She turned back towards the inside of her flat and shouted: 'What was the name of that girl who moved out recently?'

'That girl Holubová?' I heard a shaky, elderly, male voice.

'That's it, Holubová,' said the woman. 'Holubová was her name, but she doesn't live here any more.'

'Any idea where I might find her?'

'Some hope!' said the woman.

'Not even at her place of work?'

'Well, if she ever did any work. Except maybe at night; now if you crawled through all those dingy dives down in Libeň you might possibly find her.'

Had she actually deceived me even about her name? Or had she deceived this woman here and was merely testing me?

The thought stayed with me for a long time: that everything which had happened had only been some special trial, whose sense I couldn't fathom, and which I'd never know whether or not I'd passed.

A few years later – my father had long returned from prison, the Generalissimo's body had been removed from the Mausoleum and I had a job as an editor – I had some time to kill before my evening train and so I dropped into the Srdíčko wine bar.

She was sitting at a table with an elderly man. She had a different hair-do and of course different clothes but she was as brilliantly colourful as ever and her face had hardly changed. She, too, recognized me instantly, acknowledged my greeting with a smile, and then I saw her explaining something to her companion. A moment later she got up and on high heels came tripping over to me.

'Have you got a little while?' I asked.

'Difficult now. As you see . . . '

'I only have a few minutes now, too, I have a train to catch. I looked for you that time. But they told me you'd moved out.'

'Had to. They instructed me to.'

Suddenly I was back in another time, in other circumstances. 'And how did that business end?'

She placed her finger on her lips.

'I'd very much like to see you. Think you can make some time for me?'

'You'd like to come and see me, pet?' Then she said, all right, why didn't I come. Maybe Saturday evening. Or whenever I wanted. She was now living in the Vinohrady district, in Makarenko Street, Number 23, first floor, she was a subtenant of a Mrs Rotterová. Tall, dark-brown front door, with a crucifix over it. I must ring hard because her room was right at the back of the flat and she could only just hear the bell.

I put all the details down in my notebook. And her name was still the same?

Why shouldn't it be? No, she hadn't got married if that's what I meant.

On Saturday, before dusk, with a bunch of carnations in my hand, I took the tram to Vinohrady. I had no difficulty finding Number 23 on Makarenko Street. The door on the first floor was low, yellow, and there was no crucifix over it, nor anything else. No one in the building knew any Mrs Rotterová. Just as they didn't know any Mrs Slepičková or any Miss Holubová.

I tried the houses on either side but I knew in advance that I wasn't going to find her in that street.

The Tightrope Walkers

It was a rather overcast, blustery early evening in July when I arrived at Ota's wooden weekend cottage on my ancient Eska bicycle. The cottage stood in the bend of a river which at that moment looked like a tranquil little stream. The water lapped against the stony banks and the aspen leaves rustled softly. The spot was so full of peace and ease that it conjured up the images of my dead friends. Here I was listening to those gentle sounds, while they had long been enveloped in silence.

Perhaps it was the result of my wartime experiences or of a self-pity typical of my age, but I had never quite been able to surrender to pleasure or joy, or to relax. As if I never ceased to be aware of the connection between happiness and despair, freedom and anxiety, life and ruin. My feelings were probably those of a tightrope walker on his high wire. No matter how fixedly I was looking upwards I was still conscious of the drop below me.

I had only once in my life seen tightrope walkers. That was less than a year after the war. They'd come in four horse-drawn caravans, and on the open ground in our street – that is where the town actually ended then, because beyond there were only cemeteries and army training grounds – they'd put up three masts. One of them was so high I felt giddy merely looking up at it from the ground. Between the two lower ones they stretched the wire, and below that they suspended a net. On the upper platforms of the masts they then laid out a lot of props: various bicycles, a two-legged table and one-legged chairs, an umbrella, a hoop and those long balancing poles that tightrope walkers use.

I couldn't wait for the performance to start and so I was one of the first to arrive. I chose a spot on a hard-trampled heap of clay, from where, I assumed, there'd be the best view, and peered up. I was aware of a vibration of the wire, the tall mast was visibly swaying from side to side. Then the gigantic searchlights were turned on and the loudspeakers came hoarsely to life. A moment later a girl in glittering blue clothes, with hair as dark as coal and a heart-stoppingly beautiful face, stepped up to me and held out a little collecting-box. I gave her a ten-crown note and she smiled charmingly at me: with her lips, her face and her eyes. Then she flicked her head back so that the band in her hair flashed for a moment as if it was on fire, and tore off a ticket for me. I watched her moving lithely through the spectators and quite forgot to look forward to the performance. After a little while it began. Two tall young men rode and jumped along the high wire, passed one another, about-turned, juggled, and even turned somersaults, but I still wasn't so gripped that my eyes wouldn't from time to time sweep the crowd of spectators in search of that gorgeous creature. But I'd lost sight of her, all I saw was a sea of faces turned skyward. Then the two chaps came off the wire, there was a drum roll from below and at last I saw her, the beautiful girl, now in a short, silvery skirt and a close-fitting, sleeveless, silvery top, climbing up that third mast, the highest one, under which there was no safety net and which towered like a huge spike ready to be thrust into the black sky. Everyone around me slowly raised their heads as, together with me, they watched the silvery tightrope walker ascend, captured in a circle of light.

When she stood at the top she bowed, reached out for something, fastened something invisible, abandoned the one solid point under her feet and was suddenly in mid-air. Along with everybody else I gasped in horror, expecting a terrible crash, but she must have been holding on to a rope or perhaps a bar, so thin it couldn't be made out from the ground, though it seemed to me that the acrobat was being

136

kept in the air by some miracle or perhaps by the lightness of her body being carried by puffs of wind. In the monstrous silence which had fallen nobody dared make a move or take an audible breath, and in that silence the acrobat up there was turning ever wilder somersaults, doing handstands, standing on her head and pulling her body through loops made by her own limbs, rising like an angel, like a fiery phoenix, she was magnificent and admirable in her skill and her strength. But, while I admired her, I also felt uneasy, terrified that she might fall, and it seemed to me that this was not just my own unease, an understandable vertigo at the thought of someone else falling, but that I was experiencing her unease, that I was gripped by her vertigo, and I felt like screaming. I had to shut my eyes. I opened them only when the drums came to life again. I just caught a glimpse of her flying through a totally blank void and catching an invisible rope. Then she slid down.

The tumblers performed in our street for four days running, and during that time I watched every single performance.

My savings were swallowed up to the last cent but I had no regrets. The moments when I came face to face with her, when the clinging gaze of her dark eyes rested on me, as I offered her a ten-crown note, and from her long strong fingers accepted the tiny slip of paper, flooded me with a happiness that lasted me for the rest of the day. I dreamed of speaking to her, of telling her how I admired her, how I shared in her vertigo. Needless to say, I never summoned up enough courage.

On the fifth day I saw the men cram the masts and their equipment into the caravans and harness the horses. I knew that I should ask them where they were making for, but at the same time I realized that their answer would have been no use to me. I had no money left to pay for admission to another performance, and I lacked the skills and the courage to offer to travel with them. There wasn't a single drop of circus blood in me and quite certainly not the slightest talent for tightrope walking. So I just took up my place on the heap of clay and waited in case she looked out of a window. I was determined to wave to her. Or even to blow her a kiss. But the caravans drove off and I didn't see her again.

I kept thinking about her for a long time.

What, I wondered, did she dream of as she climbed up the mast for her *pièce de résistance*? Of a solid net under her? Of a mast so low that one might safely jump down at the moment of fatal vertigo? Or of having wings?

But who'd get excited about acrobatic acts on a stunted mast? Who'd be interested in a girl acrobat with wings? If she began to dream about wings she'd only be dreaming of her ruin. That's when I saw the connection between heights and vertigo, ecstasy and ruin, soaring and falling.

Ota and I had been classmates ever since the third form. After finishing school he studied engineering and I philosophy, and so we drifted apart. But at school we'd been friends, and the last year at school we'd shared a bench. Our temperaments and gifts were suitably complementary: I tended to be melancholic, agonizing over such problems as life after death and the existence of God, and also over how to build a better world, but he was not disturbed by any such things. He was sure that one day man would work everything out mathematically, including how the world began and how it should be arranged to make life on it better straight away. He got me to correct his essays and copied my Latin compositions, while I cribbed his physics homework and science tests.

Anyway, he'd invited me to this cottage many times but I had never taken up his invitation. This year he'd sent me a card again urging me to come. Under his signature there had been a note in a strange hand: 'Be sure to come, I'm looking forward to it a lot, Dana.'

How could someone be looking forward to my coming if they'd never seen me in their lives?

I leaned my bike against the rim of the well. It felt odd

138

being here: in front of a strange house in an unfamiliar countryside. I have always been anxious not to be a burden to anybody. And on top of it all he had his girl here.

So why had they invited me?

I pulled the string, and at the far end of it something rang. Inwardly I hoped they wouldn't be at home so I could quickly ride away again.

The door was opened by a thin girl with black hair and dark eyes in an unseasonably pale face. From the face, a long sorcerer's nose projected expressively. For a moment she looked at me in astonishment, then she smiled: why of course, she knew me from a photograph and from Ota's account. Besides, ever since this morning she'd had a feeling I would come this very day.

How could she have had a feeling someone would come whom she'd never seen in her life?

Ota and I took a walk along the river while his girl friend promised to get a meal ready for us.

The whole way he talked about her. She was younger than us, had only just finished school, but it seemed to him as if it was the other way about, by her side he felt uneducated, uninteresting and immature – maybe also because she'd been through a lot of ghastly things in her life or because there was in her something he couldn't put a name to. The nearest word he could think of was 'clairvoyant'. Maybe I'd be interested to know she also wrote poetry. It was very odd. I probably remembered he never thought much of poetry, but her poems, he had to admit, seemed to him interesting.

I asked what ghastly things she'd been through.

During the war both her parents had been executed and she herself had been dangerously ill. No, by then the war had been over, that had been recently. Meningïtis – that's why she was so pale and wasn't allowed out in the sun. If I asked her, maybe she'd show me her poems. He'd be interested to know what I thought of them.

When we got back she was standing by the cooker frying

139

potato pancakes. The table was perfectly laid: cutlery, plates, glasses and napkins.

We sat down and she began to bring in the food. Her cheeks were now flushed and whenever she passed by me I thought I could feel the glow that was emanating from her. We praised the food and she smiled at me and Ota, but when she looked at him it was a different kind of smile: with an inner light to it, a smile full of kisses.

I couldn't get rid of the feeling that I was in the way. I stuck out like a sore thumb, like a boulder in a field. No one here needed me. If only I had had a girl to bring along.

Why was I always alone? Was I not worthy of attention or love? Surely there had been times when I felt exceptional, destined for some glorious, unrepeatable achievement: countless ideas, incidents, destinies and images were chasing one another in my mind. But who would suspect it of me? I'd never been able to overcome my shyness, not even in my writing. Those few stories which I'd so far had published revealed nothing of all the grand goings-on inside my mind.

Perhaps she noticed my taciturnity because she suggested we might go outside and light a fire.

The wind had dropped almost completely, the night sky was clear, except over the river where there still hung some narrow half-transparent streaks of mist. We collected some wood and the fire was soon going well. The flame illuminated the branches of the trees from below, and also those two as they sat side by side, happy to be close to each other. How many similar fires were at that moment burning in the furthest corners of the earth – harmless, friendly fires? But one day they might fuse together into one single, searing, white flame that would run across the earth in a single flash, melting the rocks and turning the air red-hot. What would be left then?

I felt sorry for the world, and also for myself at the thought of melting in that fierce heat, of not being able to escape, no, I wouldn't succeed a second time. I was aware that, in spite of the heat from the fire, there was again the chill breath of death at my back. If I turned my head I might perhaps catch sight of it. I suspected that it bore no resemblance to that skeletal monster with empty eye-sockets and a scythe over its shoulder: it had a starry face and its wings, even at the slightest trembling, would block out the sun like a thick cloud. Through its mouth flowed a river that had neither beginning nor end, it was a river I would like to sail down, gazing at its banks, but it was a river I would be sailing till the end of time and whose banks I wouldn't see again.

I was aware that she was watching me.

'Let's sing something?' she suggested.

Ota got up to fetch his guitar and the two of us were left alone. She asked if something had happened to me.

No, nothing at all.

What had I been thinking of?

That I couldn't say. I really couldn't.

Had I been thinking of somebody, of somebody close?

No, I hadn't been thinking of anybody. Not of anybody in particular.

Had I been thinking about death?

What made her say that?

She wouldn't want me to think of such things. At least not that evening.

Was she really clairvoyant? I didn't know what to say. I rose to my feet and chucked some more logs on the fire. A column of sparks shot skyward and quickly died away like falling stars.

She would like me to feel happy here. Was there anything I'd like her to do for me?

No, I was entirely content.

I was merely trying to make her believe that. Why didn't I tell her what I wanted most of all at that moment.

I was silent.

But I must answer spontaneously.

No, I couldn't do that!

Why not?

I couldn't say it out loud.

By why not? She, for instance, would like to be able to love someone. Completely and without reservation.

But wouldn't she like even more for someone to love her?

She shook her head. A person who accepted love was like a passenger. Maybe on a boat, at night, on some vast lake. Whichever way you looked there was nothing but calm black water. It was true that the water might rise and swamp you. But to love someone meant to fly, to rise above the earth yourself. So high that you could see everything. Even if the world looked different from that height, even if it looked changed, even if what on the ground seemed important was transformed into insignificance. She'd say, moreover, that you could always get out of a boat and go ashore, but from that height you could only crash.

When we went inside again I asked her for her poems and she lent me an exercise book. They'd put me up in a tiny room which contained only a hat-stand, a bed, a little table and a candlestick with a candle.

I lit the candle and read for a while from her exercise book. Her poems abounded in images that were difficult to understand: timid violets, cobalt depths, glances of mournful souls, stars that had died and the healing nature of friendly lakes. Now and again between the pages I found a pressed flower with a pungent fragrance.

The next morning, immediately after breakfast, I thanked them for their hospitality and said goodbye. She squeezed my hand. She was glad she'd made my acquaintance and she hoped we'd meet again soon.

I mounted my bicycle. They were standing in front of their little cottage, holding hands and seeing me off like a happy, loving married couple.

About two months later she dropped in on me.

She was wearing a suit, her hair was carefully groomed and she was wearing lipstick. She blushed when she saw me. Her dark-brown eyes looked at me mournfully.

She happened to be walking past, returning from Ota's, and she suddenly thought she might drop in.

I couldn't understand why she'd visited me. Had anything happened to Ota?

No, nothing. Nothing at all. She'd been walking past and she just thought she'd look to see if I really lived here. And now she'd be off again.

I asked her in but she refused to enter my flat. Her cheeks were flushed as if she were feverish.

'You're sure nothing's happened?'

She shook her head. Ota was great. He was the best person she could imagine. But she had to go now.

I said at least I'd see her to the tram.

She wasn't taking the tram, she only lived a short distance away, by the park behind the water tower.

I walked with her down a narrow little street between villas. Dusk was beginning to fall, a cloudless September evening, the gardens fragrant with foliage and with roses past their peak.

I learned that she was living with a distant aunt here in Prague. But she had been brought up by her grandmother. Her grandmother had looked after her from the time they'd taken her parents away, and she'd looked after her better than anyone else could possibly have done. But last summer she'd died. Soon afterwards she herself had caught virus encephalitis and it had really seemed as if she'd follow her family, but that wasn't to be yet. Ota had been marvellous during that time. When she'd been a bit better he'd sat with her in the garden and read to her, because she was forbidden to read. If the doctors had had their way they'd have forbidden her to think too, because thoughts were sometimes painful, and hers were continually drifting over to the other side, into the darkness, where her dear ones were. Or else to the divide, to the edge, to the moment when everything collapsed. She kept imagining the moment when they were called by name, when they were led in perfect health down a corridor into

143

a room where there was nothing except tiles, and then a machine for . . .

Her voice shook. She wouldn't talk about it any more. She knew from Ota that I'd been there too. That I'd been through something similar. She'd wanted to ask me about it but she wasn't sure she wouldn't be hurting me, because it must be terrible to think back to those days, and no doubt I'd much rather forget all about it and it was silly of her to hark back to it.

I said I wasn't trying either to remember or to forget; I believed that even the most terrible experiences, provided a person got over them, could in retrospect become their very opposite.

And if a person didn't survive them?

I did not understand her question.

Weren't the souls of those people marked permanently by their frightful experiences?

I gasped. No such question had ever occurred to me. Which was odd, considering I often reflected on the existence of the human soul, and considering so many of my relations and friends had come to a similar end, standing – how did she put it? – at the divide, on the edge from which they hurtled down, who could tell where.

I said that death, surely, was always a fall and that violence was always done to the body of him who died. But if we believed in the immortality of the soul then it followed that we also believed in its ability to free itself from suffering, from the fall of the body.

And did I believe in that immortality? After everything I'd been through? That's what she wanted to know – if, after all that, it was still possible to believe.

I shrugged. I dared not say No.

And the people back there – she wouldn't say any more after that – had they believed, had they been able to believe?

I replied that some of them had – in as much as anyone could know that sort of thing about somebody else. But I remembered that at the *sukkoth* festival they had collected brushwood and built a tabernacle in the barracks yard. I also remembered a dark room in the attic where the men had met for prayers, there had been so many I thought I'd suffocate in the crowd. And I had a friend, my own age, he was dead now, we used to talk about it, and he maintained that man was in the hands of the All-Highest, that everything was happening by His will and decision, and therefore had a purpose, except that man often did not understand it and therefore questioned it and even rebelled, yes, he'd certainly believed in it all even at the moment when, as she had put, he stood at the divide.

She said she was grateful to me.

I accompanied her to the little park at the edge of which she lived; it was only a few blocks away from Ota's. The streetlamps were coming on and an evening mist was descending.

Was I sure I wasn't angry with her for delaying me so? She'd really meant to ask me what I did, what I was writing, and she'd also wanted to tell me about a book by Dos Passos which she'd just finished: she liked it, it seemed to her to be interestingly written, but she didn't want to make me even later, she hoped I didn't mind. She might bring me that book some time, or else she'd get Ota to give it to me.

As I was falling asleep and once more went over that unexpected visit in my mind, I realized that the house where I lived was quite definitely not on the way from her flat to Ota's.

About a week later I caught sight of her from my window. She was walking up and down the pavement opposite. I ran out to meet her. When she saw me she smiled at me and blushed. Her hair was curled into shiny black ringlets – clearly the hairdresser had been at work on them very recently.

She'd brought me the Dos Passos book but she'd been afraid she might be disturbing me. Perhaps I'd been writing?

She handed me the book.

Again we walked down the same little street of villas. I asked about her health.

She was feeling excellent. As recently as the summer, when I visited them, she used to get tired towards evening and find it difficult to control her thoughts; they'd be drifting through her head like clouds and at night they'd enter her dreams, such ugly dreams, but now she could control them and she seldom had any dreams now, at least not those bad ones. When they'd discharged her from hospital in the summer they'd advised her to postpone her studies for a year, but now she thought that mightn't be necessary. She'd try to attend lectures. Her grandmother agreed with her. Anyway she believed one shouldn't give up without trying and one shouldn't make things too easy for oneself. Ota, on the other hand, wanted her to take care of herself and not to study. Sometimes she had the feeling that he was jealous – jealous of anything that was not somehow connected with him. She wasn't saying this as if she was complaining about him – she'd never complain about him even if she had good cause to do so, which she hadn't, he really was the best human being she knew, but no doubt he'd change in that respect too as he matured more fully.

What did she mean? Surely he was older than her.

That wasn't the point. The real point was how a person was able completely to accept whatever life brought him. And stop making excuses. To himself and to others. But who could claim to be able to do just that? Ota was loving, perceptive and attentive. When she was ill he'd sent her flowers every day, and always different ones. What flowers did I like?

Flowers, unfortunately, were something I'd never understood. Once, it must have been in the fifth form, Ota and I had bought a guide to the local flora and had set out to the Prokopské valley. We'd succeeded in identifying a euphorbia and a tall buttercup which, however, might also have been a golden-yellow buttercup, depending on whether one regarded the stem as smooth or hairy. We couldn't agree and finally we picked the plant and showed it to our botany master, who informed us that it was a helianthemum. Since then I hadn't done any flower guessing.

Ota also spoke of me and our schooldays, but he hadn't told her that incident.

How did he speak of me?

Approvingly, always approvingly. He didn't speak ill of anybody, except that he'd warned her to be on her guard with me because I invariably tried to get off with any girl, but she was sure he didn't mean it nastily, he'd probably merely wanted to say that I had a knack with girls. She broke off abruptly and blushed.

I was stunned by my friend's statement. I said I hoped she didn't think anything of the sort.

Oh no, although she didn't really know me.

We stopped at the edge of the little park where she lived. She looked at me and I noticed the colour leaving her face.

Was anything wrong with her?

No, nothing!

Was she not feeling well?

She was perfectly well. She was better than she'd been for a long time.

I suggested that we might go for a longer walk some time and have a chat about books if she liked. If it was all right with her I'd wait for her at this spot on Sunday, straight after lunch. Unless one o'clock was too early?

I stood at the corner of the little park and watched her till she disappeared into her building. What had made me suggest that excursion? Surely I knew she was in love with someone else.

On Sunday she arrived on the dot. I asked her if she'd ever been to the Šárka Wilderness.

No, she hardly ever went walking with Ota, at most they'd go to the cinema or to a concert. That evening they were going to see *Umberto D.* Had I seen the film?

I hadn't. It was said to be good. But I had no one to go with.

147

We took a Number 11 tram to its terminus and set out towards the cliffs. Although September was nearing its end, it was a mild day and the warm yellow of the birch leaves lay poured out against a blue sky.

When I said I had no one to go to the cinema with, what did I mean?

Well, my friends all had their girls and my brother had different tastes.

She didn't want to be nosy but surely, if I wanted to, surely . . . I wouldn't have to be alone.

I'd probably not yet met a girl with whom I felt I'd want to spend my time, let alone my life.

Yes, she knew what I meant. She'd felt the same until she met Ota. When she first saw him she realized that he was that person, the right person, for her. Suddenly she blushed and added that at least she thought so at the time.

And didn't she think so any more?

She swallowed, looked at me, and shrugged. I understood her gesture. I had brought on that shrug. At that point I should have turned back, returned home, or at least been silent, or avoided talking about anything to do with emotions. But at the same time I was happy or at least pleased that she was interested in me. So we continued walking and I talked – that was the only thing I was reasonably good at then. Words and their secret power. I reflected on the advantages and disadvantages of loneliness and I knew that she would understand how I longed for love, I spoke about my wartime childhood, the lack of feeling in the world in which I had to live, and she understood that I was longing for tenderness.

She was a receptive listener. I watched my words dropping into her like some instantly sprouting seeds. Several times, as though by accident, she touched my hand. We also saw a late butterfly and rings of autumn crocuses and some shrub whose leaves were a bright fiery red. Then a small stream ran across our path. I jumped over to the far side and held out my hand to her. She gripped my fingers and jumped. She was standing so close to me that I only had to open my arms, and that's what I did. She pressed herself against me and her lips enveloped my mouth: she was kissing me, I realized, not I kissing her. One passionate kiss, then she pushed me away. She was sorry, she was terribly sorry, she didn't know what had come over her. What was she to do now? How was she to explain it?

Whom did she have to explain anything to?

Her grandmother, of course.

But she'd said, or at least I'd understood, that she was on her own now, that her grandmother had died last summer.

Yes, but surely that didn't mean she couldn't still turn to her.

We said goodbye at the edge of the park again. She whispered not to be angry with her. She didn't understand anything, she'd had no idea anything like that might happen. Because she loved Ota. Anyway, she didn't quite know what to do, how she could go to the cinema with him that evening; she only knew she mustn't hurt him.

I proposed that I would wait for her there in the park in three days' time, at six in the evening.

She thanked me for the invitation but she wasn't sure if she'd come. Perhaps I understood, I was sure to understand. She made a movement with her head as if about to kiss me but she checked herself, turned and quickly walked away.

I followed her with my eyes. What did I actually feel? Happiness? Unease? Self-satisfaction? Should I break into a run to follow her or turn and escape?

In the morning there was an envelope in the letter box for me. I immediately recognized her small, neat handwriting.

It was a sheet of paper with eight lines of poetry:

> The shades now steal over the rocks,
> my heart constricts as in a dream
> and in my head an angels' team
> sounds the alarm, a fear now rocks

and chills my wildly shaking bones:
my body still lives in this world
like a birch rooted amid stones
but, oh, my soul is downward hurled.

I had written a number of poems myself, and some of them I'd dedicated to people, but I had never yet received from anybody a poem dedicated to me. Now that I was out of reach of her mournful gaze and only her words could reach me, as tokens of her favour, I surrendered totally to a sense of happiness. I was being loved!

For the rest of the day I couldn't tear my thoughts away from her. Towards evening I set out at random for the park by the water tower. It was getting dark but, because it was a fine day, mothers with pushchairs were still moving along the neat paths. I tried to look for her window but I didn't know which of the many third-floor windows was the right one. A floor higher a young woman stood on the window-ledge, sleeves rolled up, washing the window frames. I was seized by vertigo and quickly turned away. I sat down on a park bench and waited. I shut my eyes to give her an opportunity to appear unexpectedly. She did not appear, but the woman in the window disappeared and I was flooded by a sense of loneliness. This was how I would be all my life: lonely. I'd wait for a woman who had no idea I was waiting for her because I couldn't face up to addressing her and telling her that I wanted her to come. I walked home down the little street between the villas and I could see myself lying lonely on a bed in some cold, dingy room, dying. No one knew who I was, no one loved me, I was like a stray dog, except that I was a human being who, at that moment at least, longed for another living human being; and just then I caught sight of one. I saw an angel appearing out of the heavens and floating down to my bed: a delicate, slim, sharp-nosed angel.

Back home I wrote until it was nearly midnight. I did not put myself on the bed but her – or rather a strange girl student. She was incurably sick and had been bedridden for several months. Her parents had placed her bed by the window so she could watch the branches of a massive lime-tree. Through the branches shone the blue of the sky; on clear days the sun sank amidst a reddish haze in the west. The girl had a boy friend who was a student, too, though during the last few weeks he had done virtually no work but had sat by the sick girl for hours on end, talking in order to lessen the thickening gloom of her mind. He would tell her what had happened to him during the day and whom he had met, he re-enacted the plots of films, he reproduced conversations he'd happened to overhear, and finally, when he had told her everything, he began to invent incidents and meetings, and because by then he'd become a good story-teller he invented such detail that not only she but even he himself was no longer able to tell what had really happened and what he'd dreamed up. And so he told her one day that he'd seen an angel, and that this had happened while he was walking home from her in the evening. The angel had floated up outside his window and there had been a glow coming from it.

She did not doubt the encounter, she merely said that the angel had probably visited him because he was so good to her, and he was glad she believed him: it is good for a dying person to believe in heavenly beings. After that he told her frequently of encounters with the angel. He described its appearance, its ability to turn up at any time. The angel never spoke but it inspired thoughts and filled him with a sense of bliss. She listened to him attentively, sometimes it seemed to her that she too was seeing this being, she saw it rising up above her bed or above the head of her lover, and whenever she saw the angel, she experienced a particular relief.

As the disease which consumed her spine was causing her more and more pain the girl yearned increasingly for this being. And indeed the angel would now always come to her as soon as her boy friend had left, and would spread a fine cloud of light before her, with brightly coloured reflections gyrating and spinning, merging into a continuous chain of pictures: landscapes never seen, the rise and fall of waves, the reflection of peacocks' feathers in lakes, mountain ranges, snowdrifts, or the shy eyes of animals. Such tranquillity emanated from the cloud that it quieted her suffering and all she was aware of was the calm passage of time.

Her condition worsened, the doctor held out hope for only a few more days of life and in his bag he had his morphia ampoules ready in case the pain should become unbearable. Surprisingly, however, the girl did not seem to suffer.

Then one evening, as the sun's disc was sinking behind the branches, the girl awoke feeling anxious and lonely. Her boy friend had gone a little while earlier, leaving his place to her unearthly comforter. Except that in the space between the window and the empty chair there was now no one and she looked around in vain into all the corners. And then she saw It. She gazed into starry eyes which stared from emptiness into emptiness and their glance pierced her with a chill. The girl softly cried out for her comforter. And at that moment she actually saw the angel in the window. The gentle, good, comforting being motioned with its head, and the movement was so eloquent that the girl, as though driven by some strange force, got up from her bed and with hesitant steps approached the window. When the angel saw her coming it opened its arms and stepped back a short distance. Now it no longer stood in the window but hung between heaven and earth, its translucent wings quivering in rainbow hues and its golden eyes looking at her. That glance lifted a great weight from her, she felt preternaturally light, so light she could fly. And, as she stood by the window, she opened her arms wide, rose to the narrow ledge and with a single small step pushed off upwards to follow the unearthly being into eternity, even though her body fell to the ground.

I was surprised by my own product. Until then I had written about things and about people who were either real or modelled on reality, but what was the meaning of this incident? It was nonsensical. Or did it carry a message? Had she planted it in me?

I did not know, but I managed to copy the text first thing the next morning, put it in an envelope and drop it into her letterbox.

I spent the day under the wing of my angel. I attended my lectures, somebody spoke to me and I even replied, then I walked through the city, got on a tram and got off again, but I didn't take any of this in. Only towards the evening did the world begin to get through to me the way I had become used to perceiving it: full of incident, struggle, great emotions and movements, a world of pain, passions and wars, a world whose dimensions surpassed the human mind's capacity for comprehension no matter how much we kept trying to comprehend it. And I, instead of endeavouring to discern at least its outline, had written down a crazy vision and, what was more, given it to a person whom I cared about to read. How could I now show my face to her without shame?

I had to wait for her for nearly half an hour. But she came. A little pale and with swollen eyes.

She realized she was late, it wasn't like her, but she'd wavered to the last moment about coming at all, about whether even seeing me wasn't already an act of betrayal vis-à-vis Ota. Except that she'd be thinking of me anyway. As a matter of fact, she'd been thinking of me from the moment she'd found in her letterbox the thing I had sent her; she wasn't sure what to call it, for her it was something like a parable. A parable about love and death.

We walked down little backstreets to the river. It was not yet really dark but the lamplighter with his long pole was already turning the streetlamps on. She went on talking about my story. She felt that it had come from the depths of my soul. Every single image and every sentence. She thought this was the only way one person could speak to another, touch another's soul.

Her words filled me with satisfaction. Perhaps I really had

touched her, and what more could I have hoped for? You marvellous power of words, I invoke you, I conjure you up so that I may conjure with you!

I said that she'd helped me, without her I couldn't have written anything like it. She reminded me of an angel. There was in her something other-worldly and fragile. When I was vainly waiting for her that afternoon . . .

When had I been waiting for her? Yesterday afternoon? Yes, she'd been with Ota then but she couldn't get rid of a feeling that I was within a few steps of her, that if she turned her head I'd be there; she had to say goodbye to Ota, she even asked him to leave her alone and hurried home. She'd been looking for some message from me but didn't find one until this morning! Ever since, she'd been unable to cut herself loose, even though she knew she had to drive me out, at least out of her mind. For Ota's sake and for hers.

No, she didn't have to, I implored her. Surely we weren't doing anything wrong. And I felt at ease with her. She'd no idea what it meant to me to be walking with her like this and listening to her.

Was that true?

I wouldn't say so if it wasn't!

She was glad she could mean something to me. At least for a while.

Why only for a while?

Because I would slip away from her anyway. She could feel it.

We had come along Karlova Street to the stone bridge. The lamps were casting striking patches of light on the grimy features of the saints and the windows of the Little Quarter shone like the lights of some gigantic Christmas crib.

Did she like it here?

Very much. This was the first time she'd been here at night.

But it wasn't night yet.

154

She didn't even go out in the evening. Grandmother had always wanted her to get home before nightfall.

Even in winter?

But it wasn't winter now.

But she was older now than when her grandmother died.

But grandmother was still wanting it. She worried about her. More than ever during these past few days.

'Because of me?'

We went down the steps, past some abandoned market stalls, and got to the Sova Mills.

'Not because of you. Because of me.'

We leaned against the little stone wall above the weir. The water was low and quiet. A few ducklings scurried about the dark surface. There was a smell of rotten chestnuts. She said: 'Last night I dreamed that Ota came to me in tears. Begging me not to leave him. And you were sitting there, smiling. I wanted to ask you to go away but I couldn't move my lips. Then I noticed that grandmother was sitting there too. I waited for her to advise me what to do, but she kept silent as if she couldn't open her mouth either. When I woke up I wanted her to come to me, to whisper at least one word to me – yes or no – but she kept silent. I'm sure she's angry with me.'

'Or else she thinks you're old enough now! That you must make your own decisions!'

'Yes,' she agreed, 'I realized that later. Now she'll never appear to me again . . . Got to stand on my own feet now. I've made my decision. That's why I am late; I didn't want to come until I'd made my decision.' She pressed herself against me and I could feel her lips passionately covering mine.

I was aware of a sense of almost exultant satisfaction. Simultaneously I felt some irritation that she should have made her decision without me, that she hadn't even bothered to ask for my consent. I also felt fear: fear of the fateful earnestness with which she was entrusting herself to me.

It seemed as if she were concentrating into her kiss all her love, her whole passionate being, as if she were preparing to die very shortly, entrust herself to those wings that would not bear her, and sink into the abyss. Then she stepped back from me. 'We mustn't see each other again!' Her voice struck me as painfully severe. 'If we were to see each other even once more I just couldn't bear it. Please try to understand!'

'But I thought,' I attempted an objection, 'we'd just agreed that we felt at ease together . . .'

'Please, please, don't say anything!'

'I thought,' and a wave of self-pity suddenly washed over me, 'that at last I'd found a person close to me.'

There was only the faint light of a distant streetlamp but nevertheless I thought I could see tears in her eyes.

'Perhaps some day, after a while,' she said. 'I shan't forget you. I shall never forget you.'

I was silent. Across the low, stone wall I was gazing at the river's surface on which a circular patch of moonlight was rocking. All around me and within me silence was spreading. Then suddenly, just by my legs, a heavy object hit the ground. It took me a moment to realize that it was she. She was lying on her back, arms flung out, eyes closed, a froth of saliva about her lips. I bent down over her and tried to lift her head. A horrible presentiment paralyzed me. I had invoked death and now it had come. What was I to do now?

She drew a noisy breath and opened her eyes.

'What's wrong with you, what's wrong?'

She sat up and looked about her in surprise. I helped her to her feet.

'I don't know what happened. Did I fall?' She held on to me for support.

'Let's go home, you're tired!'

'I'm all right now. Please forgive me, dearest!' She clutched my hand frantically. 'Do believe that I can't act differently. Would you act differently? A person just can't carve up his soul.'

156

I led her to the nearest seat but I clearly didn't lead her carefully enough, for when she fell again I managed only to break her fall but not to catch her.

This time she remained motionless for longer, I was unable to guess for how long, and people started to come running up.

At last she came to, some stranger helped me lift her and offered to find a taxi.

At the hospital they took her in at once. They allowed me to sit on a white bench in an empty, half-lit corridor.

She came back after about half an hour, smiling absently. It wasn't anything, she'd probably been overdoing things, they'd given her an injection and she would be all right now. I found another taxi, we were both silent during the ride, and I thought she was sleeping. In the passing light of the streetlamps she looked as pale as in a dream. Her nose projected sharply from her face like the beak of a dead bird. Hard as I tried I was unable to suppress a sense of ugliness. As if I were still hearing that gurgling sound that had come from her mouth and still seeing the froth round her sick lips. With a sudden sense of relief I realized that this girl was a stranger, that she did not belong to me nor I to her, and that fortunately we had realized this in time, that she herself had realized it and made her decision, and that I had submitted to it.

The following evening Ota turned up at our flat. He rang the bell, waited for my mother to call me, did not return my greeting and only said: 'I want to talk to you. I'll wait for you downstairs!'

The thought struck me that she might be dying after all and I was seized by terror. I quickly changed and ran outside. He was waiting for me, leaning against the trunk of an acacia.

'How is she?' I blurted out.

He did not reply but merely motioned me to follow him. We walked down the little street along which I had so recently seen her home. How many times? It had all been so shortlived – it seemed hardly worth mentioning. Except how much time did a person need to step out on to a window ledge and entrust himself to wings that would not bear him?

'She's told me everything,' he spoke up suddenly. 'You behaved disgustingly. But what else can one expect from such a . . . such a . . . ' He seemed unable to find the right word. But then he found it. 'If anything happens to her, you're a murderer.'

For the first time I entered the flat where she lived. We crossed a hall; at the far end of it he stopped me abruptly. He knocked and entered. From inside I could hear her voice but I couldn't make out the words. What did she want from me? How had she got him to bring me along? And why, if she didn't want to see me again?

At last he reappeared. 'You can go in!' He did not look at me. He stepped aside and let me enter the room behind the glass door, while he himself remained in the hall.

It was a large room, with tall walls and a stucco ceiling.

She was lying in bed, a sickly pallor on her face, a red-and-white striped duvet drawn up to her chin.

She motioned me to come closer. There was a chair by the bedside and I sat down on it. 'How are you?'

'I am absolutely fine,' her voice sounded light, almost cheerful. 'It's only that he's ordered me to stay in bed. He worries about me. I wanted to come and see you myself but he forbade me to get up. Only I had to tell you that I shall get well again. So you don't worry; this isn't ever going to happen again.

'I know you'll get well again.'

'It was all my own fault. I thought I could force myself to come to a decision and then I couldn't stand the strain. But I've come to realize that it would have been pointless anyway. I wanted you to know that I realize it now.'

I didn't understand her but before I could question her Ota walked in. 'Need anything, dear?'

'No,' she said, 'I don't want anything.'

'Got to take care of yourself, you know!' He turned to me. 'She was at death's door. The doctors said the slightest excitement could kill her. Except that some people think only of themselves. Of their own gratification.'

There was no point in defending myself. She held out her hand to me. When I took it she responded with a long and frantic squeeze. Then Ota opened the door for me and I walked out.

About three days later, as I was coming home from a lecture, I found a letter from her in our letterbox. The envelope, without a stamp or address, had only my name on it.

I tore it open as I went upstairs.

There was such a lot she wanted to say to me, she wrote, she'd wanted to do so when I visited her but there hadn't been an opportunity, so she'd tried at least to convey to me the most important thing but she wasn't now sure what she'd actually managed to say to me during that brief moment and what she'd said to me only in her mind – because she was continuously talking to me in her mind, both day and night.

She was also afraid that I might think her fickle, that I might regard her as someone who kept changing her mind. But it had all been difficult for her because she knew how much Ota loved her, and because she too regarded him highly, as a splendid, kind-hearted and self-sacrificing person. But something had occurred that she hadn't been able to imagine beforehand: she had drifted away from him, she no longer loved him. At first she'd refused to admit it to herself, she'd tried to save their relationship somehow, but then she'd come to realize that it was hopeless; love was either total or miserable, and why should she reward someone she admired, someone who had been good to her, with a love that was miserable? Why should she commit violence against herself and believe that by doing so she could make someone happy? She'd said all this to Ota, and it had been difficult for both of them because they had

159

already been preparing for a life together, but she thought he'd understood her and agreed with her decision. She didn't know what would happen now – I read with growing unease – but she felt that something had happened between the two of us, maybe beside that fire some spark had leapt across between us and lit a flame which, provided we were sufficiently wise, might burn for us always and we might spend a life together in love. She believed that we were both capable of doing so. Now she could see me in her mind's eye, my sad thoughtful eyes, my smile, beneath which she could always feel pain, and now she was waiting, waiting for my answer.

I folded the letter again and put it back in the envelope. If only I could put it back completely, put back everything that had happened, put time back.

The telephone rang. I picked up the receiver but there was silence at the other end, and all I could hear was weak breathing. I realized that she wanted to know if I'd got back home and found her message. From this moment my count-down started.

If only her letter hadn't been so totally urgent or her offer so unconditional. Did I even have the right to reject her after what I'd caused? But what feelings did I have for her? Did I have any feelings of the kind she wrote about?

Everything had happened so quickly. I wasn't able to sort out my own feelings. Maybe I could at least explain this to her. I didn't want to lose her, I was sure I'd *manage* to be fond of her, but I just wasn't ready for anything of the sort. Suppose I disappointed her? Hadn't she better reflect on whether her decision was not precipitate?

I was gripped by a fever. I had to talk to her as soon as possible. Go over it all, gain time.

I slipped on my coat and hurried along the little streets through which I'd recently walked with her. I'd yet to reach the little park, the spot where we used to say goodbye, when scraps of fairground music drifted over to me and suddenly the sky ahead was lit up by an unaccustomed glow. Then the unexpected point of a mast appeared, swaying, above the rooftops.

They had erected the masts at the edge of the little park, the high wire stretching directly above the now empty children's sandpit.

The performance was in full swing and high up I saw a spectral figure in a gleaming leotard balancing on a tall cycle, and all of a sudden I experienced that old excitement, as though I were stepping out of the damp autumn day, and I mingled with the crowd of spectators as though I had suddenly forgotten my purpose.

Was it possible that she was still with them, that for all those years, evening after evening, right to this day, my acrobat had turned her somersaults up there without crashing down?

The tightrope walker now put his bicycle aside, fetched a little table and a chair, and sat down. From the other end of the wire his girl companion approached, dressed as a waitress, a tray stacked with plates on her flat palm. I tried to make out her features but she was too high up above me. Even if she had been closer, and even if it was really her, would I still recognize her?

She was laying the plates on the little table and I was still trying to make out her features, just as though, if it were her, she might offer me some kind of salvation, just as though she might bring me some message or even some hope.

The number came to an end, the two artistes put away their props, then the man picked up a loud-hailer and turned to the spectators, inviting us to approach; he announced that he'd carry anyone among us safely on his back from one end of the wire to the other. Then he was joined by his girl companion, she too was coaxing us up on to the wire, and from her height she looked down into our dark ranks, and it seemed to me that she was looking for somebody amongst us, somebody with courage. Suddenly I realized that she was looking for me. I could feel vertigo flooding me. Yes, who else but me should go up the mast? Only what kind of figure would I cut up there, ridiculous and helpless on someone else's back? In my giddiness, would I not bring myself and my carrier down off the wire?

I looked around at the others, to see if they too had noticed that it was I who was being addressed, but they were all calmly looking upwards in the expectation of new thrills, the appeals did not concern them, they weren't even interested in whom they concerned. My feet were growing heavy. Would I even manage to climb that swinging rope-ladder up the mast?

The alluring voice appealed again to me, cut a path to me through the darkness.

I began to move in its direction but just then I caught sight of some chap in a chequered cap agilely climbing up the ladder. He'd reached the top now and was getting on to the back of the artiste in the glittering leotard.

As the two staggered across the rope there was a drum roll and I saw a slim, white figure climbing to the top of the highest mast. But it wasn't her, it wasn't a woman at all; some strange man had climbed up to the spot that had belonged to her, bowed and immediately done a handstand so that it looked as if he were trying in vain to stride across the darkness of the vast heavens.

I was watching the high-wire acrobatics, wondering if another person's anxiety and vertigo would rack me as they had once done, but I felt nothing. Either that tumbler meant nothing to me or else I was too much taken up with myself, with my own emotions. As I was standing there in the crowd, gazing up at the celestial acrobat who, high above our heads, above the dark void, was invoking that vaster one with the starry face, it seemed to me that I was beginning to understand something of the secret of life, that I would be able to see clearly what until then I had been helplessly groping for. I felt that life was a perpetual temptation of death, one continual performance above the abyss, that in it man must aim for the opposite mast even though, from

162

sheer vertigo, he might not even see it, that he must go forward, not look behind, not look down, not allow himself to be tempted by those who were standing comfortably on firm ground, who were mere spectators. I also felt that I had to walk my own tightrope, that I must myself sling it between two masts as those tumblers had done, and venture out on it, not wait for someone to invite me up and offer to carry me across on his back. I must begin my own performance, my grand unrepeatable performance. And I felt that I could do it, that I had sufficient strength in me to do it. At that moment somebody touched my shoulder. It gave me such a start I nearly cried out. But then the collecting box tinkled and before me I saw the all but forgotten, familiar stranger's face of the beautiful girl of long ago. Hurriedly I produced some coins from my pocket and gave them to her. She smiled, her teeth flashed at me in the dark and I almost felt the hot, liberating touch of her lips.

When the performance was over and the crowd had dispersed I hung about for a while in the suddenly deserted, dark, open space. Whom or what was I still waiting for?

A short distance away the eyes of a caravan shone dim yellow. Inside someone was playing a guitar and now and again a child cried noisily. I listened to this blend of sounds for a while, then I turned back home through the little streets with their gardens.

Not until the following evening did I resolve to reply: her letter had moved and surprised me, and indeed stunned me. I feared that she might have made her decision precipitately. Certainly we should meet (I was looking forward to seeing her) and talk everything over. I suggested a date, time and place (as usual, the little park outside her building). The next morning I dropped the letter in her letterbox.

It was raining on the day I had fixed. Nevertheless I got to the appointed spot a few minutes early. The tightrope walkers had gone; small heaps of disturbed soil marked the spots where their masts had stood.

I sheltered under a tall spruce, listened to the rustle of the rain in the autumn branches and watched her building; there was a light in one of the third-floor windows but I wasn't sure if it was really hers. I stared at it in the hope that I might catch some movement, the flapping of a wing, the flash of a soothing, understanding glance, but the window glowed emptily and without a sign of life, as though some will-o'-the-wisp were burning behind it.

My recent resolution evaporated. Suppose I spent my whole life just waiting, waiting for the moment when at last I saw that starry face? It would turn its glance on me and say: You've been incapable of accepting life, dear friend, so you'd better come with me! Or, on the other hand, it might say: You've done well because you knew how to bear your solitude at a great height, because you were able to do without consolation in order not to do without hope!

What would it really say?

At that moment I could not tell.

FOR THE BEST IN PAPERBACKS, LOOK FOR THE

In every corner of the world, on every subject under the sun, Penguin represents quality and variety – the very best in publishing today.

For complete information about books available from Penguin – including Puffins, Penguin Classics and Arkana – and how to order them, write to us at the appropriate address below. Please note that for copyright reasons the selection of books varies from country to country.

In the United Kingdom: Please write to *Dept JC, Penguin Books Ltd, FREEPOST, West Drayton, Middlesex, UB7 0BR*.

If you have any difficulty in obtaining a title, please send your order with the correct money, plus ten per cent for postage and packaging, to *PO Box No 11, West Drayton, Middlesex*

In the United States: Please write to *Dept BA, Penguin, 299 Murray Hill Parkway, East Rutherford, New Jersey 07073*

In Canada: Please write to *Penguin Books Canada Ltd, 2801 John Street, Markham, Ontario L3R 1B4*

In Australia: Please write to the *Marketing Department, Penguin Books Australia Ltd, P.O. Box 257, Ringwood, Victoria 3134*

In New Zealand: Please write to the *Marketing Department, Penguin Books (NZ) Ltd, Private Bag, Takapuna, Auckland 9*

In India: Please write to *Penguin Overseas Ltd, 706 Eros Apartments, 56 Nehru Place, New Delhi, 110019*

In the Netherlands: Please write to *Penguin Books Netherlands B.V., Postbus 3507, NL–1001 AH, Amsterdam*

In West Germany: Please write to *Penguin Books Ltd, Friedrichstrasse 10–12, D–6000 Frankfurt/Main 1*

In Spain: Please write to *Alhambra Longman S.A., Fernandez de la Hoz 9, E–28010 Madrid*

In Italy: Please write to *Penguin Italia s.r.l., Via Como 4, I-20096 Pioltello (Milano)*

In France: Please write to *Penguin France S.A., 17 rue Lejeune, F-31000 Toulouse*

In Japan: Please write to *Longman Penguin Japan Co Ltd, Yamaguchi Building, 2–12–9 Kanda Jimbocho, Chiyoda-Ku, Tokyo 101*

A CHOICE OF PENGUIN FICTION

The Captain and the Enemy Graham Greene

The Captain always maintained that he won Jim from his father at a game of backgammon...'Greene's extraordinary power of plot-making, of suspense and of narration ... moves continuously both in time and space and in emotion' – Angus Wilson in *The Times*

The Book and the Brotherhood Iris Murdoch

'Why should we go on supporting a book which we detest?' Rose Curtland asks. 'The brotherhood of Western intellectuals versus the book of history,' Jenkin Riderhood suggests. 'A thoroughly gripping, stimulating and challenging fiction' – *The Times*

The King of the Fields Isaac Bashevis Singer

His profound and magical excursion into prehistory. '*The King of the Fields* reaps an abundant harvest ... it has a deceptive biblical simplicity and carries the poetry of narrative to rare heights. At eighty-five, Isaac Bashevis Singer has lost none of his incomparable wonder-working power' – *Sunday Times*

The Enigma of Arrival V. S. Naipaul

'For sheer abundance of talent, there can hardly be a writer alive who surpasses V. S. Naipaul. Whatever we want in a novelist is to be found in his books' – Irving Howe in *The New York Times Book Review*

Lewis Percy Anita Brookner

'Anita Brookner shines again ... [a] tender and cruel, funny and sad novel about an innocent idealist, whose gentle rearing by his widowed mother causes him to take too gallant a view of women' – *Daily Mail*. 'Vintage Brookner' – *The Times*

A CHOICE OF PENGUIN FICTION

Humboldt's Gift Saul Bellow

Bellow's classic story of the writer's life in America is an exuberant tale of success and failure. 'Sharp, erudite, beautifully measured ... One of the most gifted chroniclers of the Western world alive today' – *The Times*

Incline Our Hearts A. N. Wilson

'An account of an eccentric childhood so moving, so private and personal, and so intensely funny that it bears inescapable comparison with that greatest of childhood novels, *David Copperfield*' – *Daily Telegraph*

The Lyre of Orpheus Robertson Davies

'The lyre of Orpheus opens the door of the underworld', wrote E. T. A. Hoffmann; and his spirit, languishing in limbo, watches over, and comments on, the efforts of the Cornish Foundation as its Trustees decide to produce an opera. 'A marvellous finale' (*Sunday Times*) to Robertson Davies's Cornish Trilogy.

The New Confessions William Boyd

The outrageous, hilarious autobiography of John James Todd, a Scotsman born in 1899 and one of the great self-appointed (and failed) geniuses of the twentieth century. 'Brilliant ... a Citizen Kane of a novel' – *Daily Telegraph*

The Blue Gate of Babylon Paul Pickering

'Like Ian Fleming gone berserk, the writing is of supreme quality, the humour a taste instantly acquired' – *Mail on Sunday*. 'Brilliantly exploits the fluently headlong manner of Evelyn Waugh's early black farces' – *Sunday Times*

A CHOICE OF PENGUIN FICTION

The Fly in the Ointment Alice Thomas Ellis

Poor mousey Margaret doesn't look a bit like a girl who is about to be married. Perhaps, Lili speculates idly, she is marrying Syl on the rebound? This deliciously malicious comedy completes the trilogy begun with *The Clothes in the Wardrobe* and *The Skeleton in the Cupboard*.

Raney Clyde Edgerton

Raney would have thought a man could get married without getting drunk. As for the honeymoon at the Holiday Inn – no amount of advice from her aunts could have prepared her for *that*. 'Splendid … what James Thurber might have written had he lived in North Carolina' – *Washington Post*

Orders for New York Leslie Thomas

One foggy June evening back in 1942, a party of Nazi saboteurs landed in the USA. As retired war correspondent Michael Findlater turned up more about the Nazi double betrayer who led them to the electric chair, he realized that someone else still remembered 1942 – and that someone wanted him dead.

Traveller Richard Adams

General Robert E. Lee and Traveller have become the stuff of legend: a brave man and his brave steed suffering together in complete accord through the bloody campaigns of the American Civil War. Traveller's simple, vivid reminiscences draw us irresistibly back… 'His best novel since *Watership Down*' – Ruth Rendell

Adam Hardrow David Fraser

The first volume in an enthralling saga of men and war. Mobilized for France in September 1939, Second Lieutenant Adam Hardrow is ardent to prove himself in battle. But he is soon to learn about the realities of war and the men he fights it with – and their wives and daughters too…

The House of Stairs Barbara Vine

'A masterly and hypnotic synthesis of past, present and terrifying future
... both compelling and disturbing' – *Sunday Times*. 'Not only ... a
quietly smouldering suspense novel but also ... an accurately atmos-
pheric portrayal of London in the heady '60s. Literally unputdownable'
– *Time Out*

Summer People Marge Piercy

Every summer the noisy city people migrate to Cape Cod, disrupting
the peace of its permanent community. Dinah grits her teeth until the
woods are hers again. Willie shrugs and takes on their carpentry jobs.
Only Susan envies their glamour and excitement – and her envy swells to
obsession... 'A brilliant and demanding novel' – *Cosmopolitan*

The Trick of It Michael Frayn

'This short and delightful book is pure pleasure ... This is a book about
who owns the livingness of the living writer; it is funny, moving, intricately
constructed and done with an observant wisdom' – Malcolm Bradbury.
'Brilliantly funny, perceptive and, at the death, chilling' – *Sunday
Telegraph*

Your Lover Just Called John Updike

Stories of Joan and Richard Maple – a couple multiplied by love and
divided by lovers. Here is a portrait of a modern American marriage in all
its mundane moments as only John Updike could draw it.

The Best of Roald Dahl

Twenty perfect bedtime stories for those who relish sleepless nights,
chosen from his bestsellers – *Over to You, Someone Like You, Kiss Kiss*
and *Switch Bitch*.

FOR THE BEST IN PAPERBACKS, LOOK FOR THE 🐧

PENGUIN INTERNATIONAL WRITERS

Gamal Al-Ghitany	**Zayni Barakat**
Wang Anyi	**Baotown**
Joseph Brodsky	**Marbles: A Play in Three Acts**
Shusaku Endo	**The Samurai**
	Scandal
	Wonderful Fool
Ida Fink	**A Scrap of Time**
Miklós Haraszti	**The Velvet Prison**
Ivan Klíma	**My First Loves**
	A Summer Affair
Jean Levi	**The Chinese Emperor**
Harry Mulisch	**Last Call**
Cees Nooteboom	**A Song of Truth and Semblance**
Luise Rinser	**Prison Journal**
Anton Shammas	**Arabesques**
Josef Škvorecký	**The Cowards**
Tatyana Tolstoya	**On the Golden Porch and Other Stories**
Elie Wiesel	**Twilight**
Zhang Xianliang	**Half of Man is Woman**

PENGUIN INTERNATIONAL WRITERS

Baotown Wang Anyi

One of China's foremost young writers draws on the stories and characters of the remote village where she was exiled during the Cultural Revolution, portraying peasant life with the vividness of a Chinese Gorky. 'This is an immemorial China of superstition, starvation and subsistence ... Here we have some of the same studied parochialism as in [Jane] Austen' – *Literary Review*

Marbles: A Play in Three Acts Joseph Brodsky

Imprisoned in a mighty steel tower, where yesterday is the same as today and tomorrow, Publius and Tullius consider freedom, the nature of reality and illusion and the permanence of literature versus the transience of politics. In a Platonic dialogue set 'two centuries after our era' in ancient Rome, Nobel prizewinner Joseph Brodsky takes us beyond the farthest reaches of the theatre of the absurd.

Scandal Shusaku Endo

'Spine-chilling, erotic, cruel ... it's very powerful' – *Sunday Telegraph*. '*Scandal* addresses the great questions of our age. How can we straddle the gulf between faith and modernity? How can humankind be so tender, and yet so cruel? Endo's superb novel offers only an unforgettable bafflement for an answer' – *Observer*

A Summer Affair Ivan Klíma

David Krempa, a biologist in Prague, and married, lives for his work. Iva, young and crazy, lives only for the moment. Their affair was madness, but once it had begun there was no going back. 'Short and sharp ... it leaves one breathless' – *Literary Review*

A Scrap of Time Ida Fink

'A powerful, terrifying story, an almost unbearable witness to unspeakable anguish,' wrote the *New Yorker* of the title story in Ida Fink's award-winning collection. Herself a survivor, she portrays Poland during the Holocaust, the lives of ordinary people in hiding as they resist, submit, hope, betray, remember. 'A masterpiece ... we are brought as close to the Holocaust as it is possible for literature to take us' – Alan Sillitoe

FOR THE BEST IN PAPERBACKS, LOOK FOR THE 🐧

PENGUIN INTERNATIONAL WRITERS

On the Golden Porch and Other Stories Tatyana Tolstaya

'There are thirteen stories in this collection and every one's an absolute gem of emotion ... It's not hard to see why quite so much fuss is being made over Tatyana Tolstaya' – *Time Out*. 'With one collection ... she has established herself as a new and original force in Russian literature in her own right' – *Mail on Sunday*

A Song of Truth and Semblance Cees Nooteboom

Two writers meet in an Amsterdam arts club, drink wine, skirt nervously around any talk of their own work and argue about the nature of fiction. For one of them, a floating pair of epaulettes is on the point of fleshing into Georgiev, a nineteenth-century Bulgarian colonel. The banal and irritating phrase 'the colonel falls in love with the doctor's wife' itches at the back of his mind...

Half of Man is Woman Zhang Xianliang

'The gulag literature of the Soviet Union is world-famous, but China's equivalent is almost unknown. *Half of Man is Woman* is exceptional not only for belonging to this genre but also – in China – for daring to make sexuality its theme, together with politics, freedom and identity' – *Observer*

The Velvet Prison Artists Under State Socialism Miklós Haraszti

'A fascinating account of totalitarian aesthetics ... he describes a culture where the traditional antagonism between censor and artist has been replaced with a strange form of collusion. In this new relationship all censors and most artists are entangled in a mutual embrace. This is the "velvet prison"' – *Guardian*

Last Call Harry Mulisch

'Intricately rewarding ... Uli Bouwmeester, an obscure former vaudeville actor, wartime collaborator and member of a famous stage family, is unearthed to play Prospero in a version of *The Tempest* that is also a play-within-a-play about the swansong of a famous actor ... who nurses a guilty secret like the old man playing him...' – *Guardian*

A Summer Affair

Their affair was madness, but once it had begun there was no going back. David Krempa, a biologist in Prague, lives for his work. His wife and children and the other pleasures of life are pushed aside by his search for the secret of human longevity. Until the day he meets Iva. Young, crazy, she lives only for the moment. Rationally Iva holds no interest for him; she treats his love with indifference and thinks only of clothes, dancing and lovers. Yet David is drawn to her sensuous, childlike world by a passion that he does not understand and, ultimately, is powerless to control.

'Short and sharp ... it leaves one breathless ... [It] is not only about an affair, but about ageing and breakdown, the framework of shocking death, the sense of loss and being lost' – *Literary Review*

'Deeply felt' – *Sunday Telegraph*

'His writing is remarkable for its refreshingly naïve style and his ability to capture a mood or emotion with the barest of words ... a powerful novel' – *Time Out*

Love and Garbage

The narrator of Ivan Klíma's novel has temporarily abandoned his work-in-progress – an essay on Kafka – and exchanged his writer's pen for the orange vest of a Prague road-sweeper. As he works, he meditates on Czechoslovakia, on Kafka, on life, on art and, obsessively, on his passionate and adulterous love affair with the sculptress Daria. Gradually he admits the impossibility of being at once an honest writer and an honest lover, and with that agonizing discovery comes a moment of choice.

'Few writers have the invention and skill to juxtapose within one novel so many diverse themes, mundane and sublime, savage and compassionate, held in a satisfying balance. He tosses time and space about in a net seeking to catch the eternal ... It is rare that one meets a new literary voice of such originality and mastery' – *Observer*